FOLLOW McLEAN

Inspector McLean is an experienced, resourceful detective whose cases are often baffling at first, but he always tracks down the criminals. He proves his ability as a sleuth who is both human and ingenious in this variety of cases.

Amongst the many crimes is the murder of a motorist on the Lymington ferry, and of a dead girl whose body was found in a river. Throughout, motives for murder are explored and murder weapons examined, including a heavy silver candlestick and a humble sparrow's nest.

FOLLOW McLEAN

George Goodchild

·BLACK·
DAGGER
·CRIME·

First published 1961
by
Jarrolds Publishers Ltd.

This edition 2002 by Chivers Press
published by arrangement with
the author's estate

ISBN 0 7540 8607 0

Copyright © 1961 by George Goodchild

British Library Cataloguing in Publication Data available

Printed and bound in Great Britain by
Bookcraft, Midsomer Norton, Somerset

8196

1

THE woman who presented herself at Inspector McLean's office, following a telephone call to Scotland Yard, was of outstanding beauty and elegance. She had given her name as Mrs. Denise Wilmot and from her speech and accent was obviously of French origin. McLean judged her age to be round about thirty, and he already knew the kind of trouble she was in.

'Tell me about your husband' he said. 'When did you last see him?'

'It was two days ago – on Wednesday evening. He arrive home from business, veri tired, and was about to have a meal when the telephone ring. I am in the kitchen but I hear him go to the telephone in the hall. I do not hear what he say, but a leetle later he come to me and tell me he must go out at once. I ask him why he cannot stay and have his dinner first, but he shake his head and go.'

'And never came back?'

'No. Yesterday I wait for some explanation, but I hear nothing. Now I am afraid something must have happen to him.'

'Did you not hear anything of the conversation over the telephone?'

'Nothing at all. The radio was on in the kitchen, and I shut the door so as not to bother him.'

'What is your husband by profession?'

'He is a partner in his brother's business in Leadenhall Street. It is called Wilmot Brothers, and they import gowns and ladies' underwear from France. His brother is in Paris now, choosing the new fashions. I was a dress model in Paris before I met my husband Edward.'

'How long have you been married?'

'Six years.'

'You know of no possible reason why your husband should suddenly go off like that?'

'None at all. I telephone his brother, Jacob, last night, and he advise me to get in touch with the police. He say he will be home this evening.'

'Where do you live?'

'Number sixteen Western Avenue, Highgate.'

'And your brother-in-law?'

'Number fourteen Panding Lane, Hampstead.'

'Have you a recent photograph of your husband?'

She nodded and delved into her handbag, to extract a very clear photograph of herself with a good-looking tall man of about her own age. It was taken outside an hotel at some southern holiday resort.

'Nice?' asked McLean.

'No – Cannes, two years ago.'

'Has your husband any financial troubles to your knowledge?'

'Oh, no. The business is prosperous. It does better and better every year.'

'Tell me what clothing your husband was wearing when he left home.'

She gave him very precise details of her husband's attire, even to the pattern and colour of his tie, all of which Sergeant Brook took down in shorthand. Finally McLean promised to look into the matter without delay, and Mrs. Wilmot thanked him and was shown out.

McLean followed the usual procedure in such cases – checking up the casualty lists in the Metropolitan area, but nothing came of it, and then, barely two hours after Mrs. Wilmot had left, she rang up, in a state of great excitement, to say that she had received an extraordinary message over the telephone. It was of such a nature that she thought it unwise to come again to Scotland Yard.

'I'll come and see you,' said McLean.

At once he and Brook drove to Highgate. They found Western Avenue completely void of traffic, but McLean left the car short of the house where Mrs. Wilmot lived, and walked from there to No. 16. Mrs. Wilmot herself opened the door, and took them into a large and well-furnished sitting-room. She was now wearing a different frock but looked no less attractive.

'Well, Mrs. Wilmot, what was the message you received?'

'It was a man talking slowly and deliberately. He say my husband is quite well, and that I am not to do anything – go to the police, or tell a soul – until I hear again

6

from him. If I do he say he cannot guarantee my husband's safety.'

'What did you say to that?' asked McLean.

'I ask him when I shall hear again, and he say it will be very soon. Then he ring off.'

'It looks very much like a kidnapping business. If you hear from him again I want you to communicate with me immediately.'

'Yes – I understand.'

'Is your husband's brother home yet?'

'I don't know. I expect he will come by air. Shall I ring him?'

'Please don't bother. I'll probably call on him on my way back. Don't forget – if there is a demand for a ransom, play for time.'

Mrs. Wilmot nodded confusedly, and McLean and Brook went back to the car, after making sure that nobody was loitering near it. Later they arrived at Jacob Wilmot's house, where they were informed by the housekeeper that Wilmot had just arrived from London Airport. McLean gave his name and was subsequently shown into the sitting-room where Wilmot was seated by a tea-tray. He was a well-built man of about forty.

'Is it about my brother, Inspector?' he asked eagerly. 'I was just about to telephone his wife.'

'Yes. Your sister-in-law reported the matter to us this morning, but since then there has been a development. It looks very much as if your brother has been kidnapped.'

Wilmot stared incredulously.

'What on earth for?' he asked.

'For a ransom presumably. Your sister-in-law was rung up on the telephone a short while ago, to be informed that here husband was quite safe, and that she would hear again soon.'

'But did they ask for money?'

'No. But there's little doubt they will before long.'

'What an extraordinary thing! I should have thought that Ted was a bit too old in the tooth to let that happen to him. He was always a tough sort of guy.'

'One isn't always given the opportunity to be tough. It seems that he was lured from his home by a telephone call of some urgency, as he left his dinner to respond to

7

it. Do you know anyone who might seek to make money in that way?'

'I don't. As a matter of fact my brother has a rather extravagant wife, and lives up to the last penny of his income. I doubt very much whether he could find any considerable sum of money in an emergency. What are we to do?'

'Nothing,' said McLean. 'If any approach is made to you by the kidnappers have nothing to do with it, but leave the matter in our hands.'

Wilmot thought for a moment.

'I suppose this is genuine?' he asked. 'Not some sort of silly practical joke?'

'People don't usually carry jokes that far. But no doubt we shall be in a position to decide that when there is another communication. It is no easy matter to collect ransom even when people are prepared to pay. They may slip up in trying to solve that little problem. Your duty is clear – to inform us of any demands either by telephone or letter.'

'You mean they might expect me to pay?'

'They might, in view of the relationship, and if they knew that your brother's wife had not the means.'

Wilmot shook his head determinedly.

'I won't play,' he said. 'The last time I went on a buying trip my brother left the office unlocked over the whole week-end and we were burgled. He got himself into this mess, and he'll have to get himself out of it.'

II

The day passed without any further communication from Mrs. Wilmot or her brother-in-law, and on the evening of the next day McLean called on Mrs. Wilmot. He found her in a curious state of nerves, and could not help suspecting that despite her denials something had happened. Then, while he was there, Jacob Wilmot called. McLean heard some whispering at the door, which confirmed his suspicions. Then Jacob came into the sitting-room, and nodded to the visitors.

'It's very curious that the kidnappers have not rung up,' said McLean. 'I suppose you have heard nothing, Mr. Wilmot?'

Wilmot looked at his sister-in-law.

'Well, have you?' asked McLean.

'You tell him, Denise,' growled Wilmot.

Mrs. Wilmot wrung her slim hands together as she faced McLean's stern gaze.

'I – I didn't tell the truth just now,' she said. 'I did hear from them – this morning. The voice said he knew I had already communicated with the police. He said that would cost me another thousand pounds. He told me that unless I paid the sum of two thousand pounds I should never see my husband again, and if I went to the police again, or told them of the call, my husband's life would pay forfeit.'

'Go on,' said McLean, grimly.

'He said I was to pack two thousand old one-pound notes in a bundle, and have the bundle placed in the first haystack on the farm which fringes the Watford By-pass just short of the Eagle Garage. The bundle was to be covered over with hay, and to be on the side off the road. It was to be delivered punctually at five o'clock today, and the person who delivered it must leave the area at once. Failure to carry out these instructions would be on my own head.'

'Nothing more?' asked McLean.

'No. He rang off abruptly. I was terrified. I had no means of getting the money. I went to see my brother-in-law. I begged him to help me, and finally he consented.'

'What else could I do?' asked Wilmot. 'I went to my bank and drew the money in used notes—'

'Oh, I forgot to tell you,' said Mrs. Wilmot. 'The voice promised me that if the instructions were carried out my husband would be back in this house at seven o'clock.'

'Well,' continued Wilmot· 'I found the place all right. There was a good deal of traffic on the road, but just near the haystack there was a farm gate, and I went through, and carried out the instructions. I saw nobody hanging about, and I got back into my car and came straight here. I'm sorry, Inspector, but my sister-in-law was so terrified there was nothing else I could humanly do.'

'You could have telephoned me,' said McLean angrily. 'That at least would have been unobserved. We could have taken action which might have resulted in the arrest of the kidnappers.'

A*—F M   9

'It was my fault,' said Mrs. Wilmot. 'I take the whole blame. I believe they would have killed my husband. I want him back safe and sound.'

'Well, he should be here in half an hour,' said McLean. 'We'll wait.'

Seven o'clock came and went, and Mrs. Wilmot's tension was enormous. By half past seven she was almost hysterical with uncontrollable anxiety.

'Steady!' said Wilmot. 'He'll be here at any moment now.'

'But I'm afraid. They may have cheated you. Perhaps Ted knew them and they dared not set him free.'

Wilmot shook his head and stared at McLean.

'What do you think, Inspector?' he asked.

'I think you've both behaved foolishly.'

A little later Mrs. Wilmot begged to be excused and went to her room. By eight o'clock Wilmot seemed to have become reconciled to the situation.

'The swine!' he muttered. 'Two thousand quid gone down the drain for nothing. Why did I ever listen to my sister-in-law?' McLean finally decided that nothing was to be gained by staying on.

'I must leave,' he said. 'I suppose you will stay here for a while?'

'Yes. I can't leave her alone in her present state.'

'Then telephone me if anything happens, at my private number.'

He handed Wilmot a card, and Wilmot nodded his head.

McLean heard nothing more that night, but the next morning Mrs. Wilmot telephoned him and told him tearfully that her husband had not returned. There was little he could do to comfort her, but before he rang off he asked for the name of her brother-in-law's bank. Later in the morning he called at the bank with Brook, and found the cashier who had cashed the cheque.

'It was a lot of money for a sudden call,' he said. 'Especially as he insisted on having used notes. But we managed to dig them up, and wrapped them in a single package in bundles of one hundred.'

'I presume there is no means at all of checking any of the notes?'

'No.'

10

'What about the wrapper?'

The cashier reflected for a moment.

'It was a printers' wrapper,' he said. 'I think it had contained a quantity of paying-in books. There was a label on the outside but I tore that off. I remember there was some blue pencilling on the end of it, done by the printer I suppose.'

'What colour was the wrapper?'

'A sort of light grey – very stout.'

McLean had to be satisfied with this very meagre information. He had hoped there might have been at least one packet of new notes, so that the numbers could be recorded and traced, but the kidnappers' instructions had been carried out all too well, and the outlook was none too promising. But where was the missing man?

III

It was ten days later that the body of a man was taken from the Thames. There was scarcely a shred of clothing left on it, and the body itself was in a shocking state. But the tightly laced shoes remained as a possible clue to identity. McLean lost no time in seeing the corpse. Immediately he realized that identification by normal means was out of the question, but he noted that the wisdom tooth on the right lower jaw was missing, and that two front teeth had recently had gold fillings. The hair was dark and under it – towards the back – was a fractured skull.

'The cause of death?' he asked the doctor.

'Yes. That was no accident. He was struck a heavy blow with a piece of metal. He was dead before he entered the water.'

McLean had the shoes dried, and then took them along to Mrs. Wilmot.

'Was your husband wearing shoes like these when he left home?' he asked.

Mrs. Wilmot took the shoes into her trembling hands.

'Yes,' she replied. 'These are his shoes. I went with him to buy them only a few months ago. He didn't like the laces that were in them, and bought that pair of thin hide ones.'

'Do you know anything about his teeth?'

'Yes. He had an impacted wisdom tooth in the bottom jaw, and had to have it cut away. More recently he fell and damaged two teeth in the front. They were crowned with gold.'

McLean, who had wanted to spare her unnecessary pain, now informed her that he believed her husband's body had been found, and that either she or her brother-in-law should attempt to identify it. Somewhat to his surprise she said she would go personally, and half an hour later she gave it as her sincere opinion that it was her husband.

After a more prolonged examination of the corpse two doctors were in agreement that death must have taken place more than ten days earlier. They favoured thirteen or fourteen days as the more likely period.

'That means he was already dead when the ransom was asked,' said McLean.

'Probably put up a resistance and was killed earlier than was planned. But where do we go from here, sir?' asked Brook.

McLean needed time to answer that question. One fact that stuck in his mind was the dead man's alacrity in responding to the telephone call. Who was it who had lured him to his death, and later had the audacity to go out for ransom? Why had he not suspected that telephone call? What plea had been put up to cause him to act so promptly, and not to confide in his wife? Was the murder planned from the start, or had it been a silly blunder on someone's part?

On the former hypothesis – who would gain from his death. The obvious answer to that was his brother, presuming the business was on a partnership basis. But the brother was in Paris at the time when the murder was committed, and it was the brother who had stepped in to pay the ransom. More information was required on that matter, and McLean went to the widow to get it.

'Did your husband leave a will?' he asked.

'No. I often asked him, but he hated wills.'

'Was the partnership on a fifty-fifty basis?'

'No. My husband was the junior partner. While he lived his interest was one-third against his brother's two-thirds of the profits. If either partner died the survivor came into full ownership of the business.'

'Then you are left unprovided for?'

'Yes, but my brother-in-law has been most kind. He has offered me a home with him, and an adequate personal guaranteed allowance.'

'Were they always on good terms?'

'Oh yes, but I must confess that it was Jacob who had the brains. The business was quite prosperous when he took his brother into it.'

But subsequent inquiries elsewhere produced conflicting evidence. Some employees of the firm stated that Jacob and Edward never did hit it off, and were always bickering, and then came a statement from a member of a Paris firm who did business with the two brothers. He said that prior to Edward's partnership Jacob had made most of the running with the beautiful model who became Edward's wife.

'That puts Jacob very much into the picture,' said McLean.

'But Jacob paid—' said Brook, and then hesitated.

'Yes, that's what we don't know,' said McLean. 'Did he really pay that money. I think we'll have a word with him.'

At the subsequent interview with Jacob McLean asked him about his recent trip to Paris.

'I left London Airport on the 18th,' said Jacob. 'And I returned on the 24th, after my wife had telephoned me at my hotel on the 23rd.'

'I should like to see your passport.'

Jacob left the room for a few moments and came back with his passport. One glance at it showed that his arrival and departure at and from Le Bourget bore out his statement. Brook seemed to think this was conclusive, but McLean noticed a photograph of a motor cruiser on the wall by the fireplace. He stepped closer to it and could recognize Jacob in the engine-pit, smiling at the photographer.

'Your boat?' he asked.

'Yes.'

'Where do you keep it?'

'At Hythe.'

'Is it there now?'

'No. I had engine trouble a month ago when I was off Paris Plage. I had to get the boat towed into harbour to have a new piston fitted. I shall run over and pick it up next week.'

McLean thanked him and left, but half an hour later he was on the telephone speaking to the French police at Le Bourget. Two hours passed before he was rung back. There was some conversation and he hung up the receiver.

'It is true his boat had engine trouble,' he said to Brook. 'But the repair was done in a week. But here's the prize bit. Wilmot took out the boat on the afternoon of the 22nd and did not return to Paris Plage until the early hours of the following morning. Altogether he was absent for ten hours – enough time to do the channel crossing both ways, and to make an appointment with his brother. On the telephone he must have warned his brother not to tell his wife, and the unsuspecting Edward went to his death.'

'But what about the telephone call demanding the ransom?'

'It came after Wilmot landed at the airport. Not difficult to disguise one's voice on a telephone.'

'There was an earlier call.'

'Yes. I think that came from France, but we have no means of checking it. I'm going to get a search warrant.'

The search at Wilmot's home revealed nothing incriminating but McLean carried the matter to Wilmot's office, with Wilmot accompanying him, and there in Wilmot's locked safe was a package done up in stout grey paper, with the printers' blue pencilling on the outside. McLean opened it and found twenty packets of old one-pound notes.

Wilmot said nothing. He seemed to realize that any sort of explanation would be a waste of breath, and soon afterwards he was formally charged with murder.

'A little too much planning,' said McLean later. 'In attempting to place himself beyond suspicion by pretending to pay the ransom he made our job considerably easier.'

'His own brother too. What some men will do for money!' said Brook.

'Not only money. I fancy he had strong hopes in another direction.'

14

2

'WENT to London Airport last night,' said Sergeant Brook, as he replaced the ribbon on his typewriter. 'My young niece is doing a cheap air-trip to Paris, and I went to see her off. Never seen such a crush there. I thought they were expecting President Eisenhower at least. But it was a bloomin' crooner on a private plane from Paris. Thousands of young teenagers mobbed him as he went to his car. It took about ten policemen to drag them away. Harry Pullinger they called him. His wife was with him, and his secretary and manager. Thousand pounds a week they said he earned. Now what has he got that I haven't?'

McLean looked up from his correspondence.

'I imagine he's got a voice, Brook,' he said. 'Or he couldn't command all that money.'

'Voice!' snarled Brook. 'Those chaps don't have voices. It's like letting the water out of your bath, and a lot of young females swallow it.'

'The bath water? It's getting a bit involved. I have a letter for you.'

The subject was killed, but a few days later McLean read an account of the crooner's spectacular success on the opening night of his London appearance.

'Your anathamatized crooner has done it again, Brook,' he said. 'A packed house, oceans of tears, twelve curtain calls, half a hundred bouquets, and a brand new song called "My Mommer has streaks of grey".'

'I must go and see him,' said Brook, with a wicked gleam in his eye. 'Do you know where I can buy some ripe tomatoes?'

But Brook's dubious intention was destined to be unfulfilled, for that evening the big music hall which had booked Pullinger for one month exhibited a notice to the effect that owing to unforeseen circumstances Harry Pullinger would not appear, and hundreds of persons who had booked seats solely to hear the world-famous crooner, demanded their money back.

The next morning there were repercussions at Scotland Yard when Mrs. Pullinger called there, accompanied by her husband's manager, in a great state of excitement, and it was McLean who was instructed to hear her complaint.

'Curious coincidence,' he said. 'Go down and bring them up, Brook.'

Mrs. Pullinger was a Hollywood type of blonde, round about thirty years of age, and inclined to plumpness. Her companion, Mr. Hatling, was a few years older. Rather wizened in appearance, and bedecked by an enormous tie, which was covered with bars of music.

'Please be seated,' said McLean.

Mrs. Pullinger sat down, but Hatling said he didn't feel like sitting.

'Now,' said McLean. 'What is the trouble?'

'I think you may have heard of my husband – Harry Pullinger, the crooner?' asked Mrs. Pullinger.

'I have indeed. I read this morning that he was unable to appear last night.'

'That's sure true,' said Mrs. Pullinger, on the verge of tears. 'At the last minute I had to phone the theatre. He just disappeared, didn't he Willie?'

Mr. Hatling, thus appealed to, unloosened his tie a fraction.

'Right into the blue,' he said. 'We have a suite at the Phoenix Hotel. I was in his room talking to him at six o'clock last evening, and he was all set to beat the first night's performance. Stupendous it was. He had 'em all hypnotized. Wal, I went back to my room to change my clothes, and a few minutes later Mrs. Pullinger came in and asked me if I had seen Harry.'

'I had been doing a bit of shopping,' explained Mrs. Pullinger. 'When I got back he was gone. We had him paged downstairs, but he wasn't in the hotel. The hall porter said he had seen him leave the hotel a few minutes before I returned. He – the hall porter – said my husband looked anxious, and was almost running. There was another man with him. We waited, and waited, and then had to telephone the theatre to say he couldn't be found.'

'Did the hall porter describe the man who was with your husband?' asked McLean.

'He said he was tall and thin, and they seemed to be going towards a car that was waiting on the other side of the street, but then the traffic stopped his view, and he didn't see what happened afterwards.'

'It's sure a frame-up,' said Hatling. 'Someone's out to get some dough.'

'Have you anything to support that argument?' asked McLean.

'No, but there's been a lot of stuff in the Press about the money he makes. He may look like a sitting duck to some sharp-shooters but if I know Harry he won't part with a dime to a gang of dirty crooks – not even to save breaking his contract.'

'We're going a bit fast,' said McLean. 'Mrs. Pullinger, do you know of any reason at all why your husband should go off like that and not return?'

'No, I don't. He's never broken a contract in his life, and always likes to rest for an hour or two before he is due at the theatre.'

'Is this his first visit to England?'

'Yes.'

'Had he been quite normal all day?'

'Oh yes, and very pleased with the reception he got the first night.'

'Can you tell me what clothes he was wearing?'

'No. He may have changed—'

'I can tell you,' said Hatling. 'He hadn't time to change from the suit he was wearing when I was with him.'

He gave very full details, and Brook recorded them in his note-book. Mrs. Pullinger had also brought a photograph which McLean retained. After promising them immediate action they were shown the door.

'Could be a stunt,' said Brook.

'To get free publicity?'

'Well, it's been done before. That fellow Hatling struck me as being a smart guy – knew all the answers.'

'I don't think Pullinger needed that sort of publicity. But we'll go along to the theatre, and see what the reaction is there.'

II

At the theatre McLean found the management in a state of acute anxiety. Pullinger's reputation in the United States, and other places had preceded him, and his enormous success on the first night had sold out the house for weeks ahead.

17

'Lord, how he puts that stuff over,' said the manager. 'If he doesn't come back at once we're in a mess.'

'What do you know of his associates?' asked McLean.

'He's got a good manager, and a hard-working secretary. The secretary told me she sent out hundreds of photographs every day. His wife thinks the world of him. If you're looking for any dirty work in that direction I think you're on a bad scent.'

'How long has he been married?'

'Six years. It was his wife who put him on the map. She does the lyrics – I mean the words – for his songs. He composes the music himself. That new song, "My Mommer", brought the house down. They screamed, they cried, they fainted. Can't understand it myself, but that's how it is.'

McLean went on to the Phoenix Hotel, and found the hall porter, who was the last person known to have seen the missing man. He could only repeat what he had told Mrs. Pullinger.

'Did you see Mr. Pullinger's companion enter the hotel previously?' asked McLean.

'No, sir.'

'Is it possible that he is staying here?'

'No, sir. I know everyone who is staying here.'

'You said they appeared to be going to a car that was parked opposite.'

'That was my impression, sir.'

'What sort of a car was it?'

'A black saloon. Rather battered I thought. The rear mudguard on the driving side was badly bashed.'

McLean and Brook went upstairs to the suite which Pullinger had reserved. It was a palatial set-up, but only the secretary was present. She was a woman in the early thirties, named Anna Hogan and she said she had been with the Pullingers for four years. In her opinion the Pullingers were happily married. She knew of no reason at all why Pullinger should suddenly rush out of the hotel with another man. She had been in this same room, changing her dress, at the time.

'Do you use this room as a general office?' asked McLean.

'Yes. My bedroom communicates with it. I take all

telephone calls here, and switch any personal calls through to the appropriate bedrooms.'

'Were there any personal calls just prior to Mr. Pullinger's disappearance?'

'Yes. One for Mrs. Pullinger. It was a man speaking. I told him that Mrs. Pullinger was out, and asked him if he would leave a message. He said he would ring again later.'

'Did he ring again?'

'No.'

McLean said he would like to see Pullinger's bedroom, and Miss Hogan took him and Brook to a magnificent room overlooking the Green Park.

'I noticed that the main door to this suite was not locked when I tried it,' said McLean. 'Is it always like that?'

'Yes – in the day time. It saves us all having separate keys. But we lock it at night.'

'So any person could have come to the door of this room, and knocked?'

'Oh yes.'

'I should like to look round.'

'Do. I shall be in my room if you want me again.'

The room was beautifully furnished, and very tidy. It had apparently not been touched since Pullinger left so suddenly, for a pair of soft leather slippers were lying close to a long chair, and on a table by the chair was an open book. There was also a half-smoked cigarette lying in an ash-tray.

'What do you make of it, sir?' asked Brook.

'All the signs are that he left in a great hurry. I think he did no more than change his footwear, and stub out the cigarette.'

'But why?'

'I'm not omniscient, my dear Brook. But at a guess I should say that the man he was seen with was the same who rang up and asked for Mrs. Pullinger. I think he rang up from close at hand, and when he heard that Mrs. Pullinger was out he came straight here and knocked on the door. Pullinger went to the door and asked him what he wanted. He must have given Pullinger some information which induced him to accompany him without delay.'

'And he had a car waiting?'

'I think so.'

'But what kind of story could he have told Pullinger to make him go off like that?'

McLean reflected for a few moments.

'I can think of one very good story,' he said. 'He had been told that Mrs. Pullinger was out. All he had to do was to pretend that Mrs. Pullinger was in some kind of trouble, and needed her husband at once.'

'That's it!' said Brook. 'Fits like a glove.'

'Yes, but it only lands us in a dead end. I wish we could get some more details about the car to which they presumably went. It must have been left somewhere over there.'

McLean stared through the window which faced the street. Immediately opposite were a few private residences, a block of flats and a tobacconist's shop.

'Go and get that hall porter, Brook,' he said.

Brook soon returned with the porter, and McLean took him to the window.

'I want you to tell me just where the car stood,' he said.

'Right in front of the tobacconist's shop,' he said. 'I was a bit surprised because no parking is allowed there.'

'Was the shop open at the time?'

'Yes, sir. It doesn't close until six-thirty.'

'Thank you.'

A few minutes later McLean was in the shop. A man and a girl were behind the counter. McLean addressed the man.

'I am a police officer,' he said. 'Were you on duty here last evening just after six o'clock?'

'Yes – both of us.'

'Did you happen to see a black saloon car parked outside for a short while?'

'No,' replied the man. 'I can't say I did.'

'I did,' said the girl. 'I was about to go out and tell the driver that he would be pinched if he was caught there, but before I could do so he had gone across the street.'

'What was he like?'

'Very tall, with a stoop. Maybe about forty years of age. He came back about ten minutes later with another man – much younger and drove away at once.'

'What sort of a car was it?'

'A very old one. I saw the number too as he drove away. It was rather a funny one – MUG 123. That's why it took my eye.'

'Thank you,' said McLean. 'You've helped quite a lot.'

Within an hour McLean's urgent inquiry was answered. The present owner of the car was a Mr. Albert Trender of an address in the higher part of Tottenham Court Road.

'Must be a flat,' said Brook. 'They are all shops in that area.

When they arrived at the address they found it was an apartment above a furniture shop. It was a corner site, and up the side street was the car in question. Some stairs beside the shop led to the apartment, and McLean and Brook ascended them and rang the bell at a door which bore Mr. Trender's card. There was a slight delay and a bald-headed man came to the door.

'Are you Mr. Albert Trender?' asked McLean.

'Yes.'

'I am a police officer, and I wish to ask you some questions regarding your car.'

'Come in,' said Trender. 'What's wrong with the car?'

McLean entered a small sitting-room, where Mr. Trender had obviously been engaged filling in football pools coupons. It was a drab sort of place.

'Did you use your car last evening round about six o'clock?' he asked.

'No. Not until seven o'clock. It was parked up the side street from four o'clock until seven.'

'Locked?'

'No. It's so old I never bother to lock it. Shouldn't mind much if someone pinched it.'

'Do you know a man named Harry Pullinger?'

'No. Who is he?'

'He happens to be a famous crooner.'

'Oh, him! Of course I've read about him, but I don't know him.'

'I have proof that your car was parked outside a shop opposite The Phoenix Hotel soon after six o'clock last evening.'

Trender opened his eyes wide.

'If it was it must have been taken without my

knowledge or permission,' he said. 'But what is the upshot of all this? Was the car involved in some accident?'

'It is believed that the man in the car kidnapped Mr. Pullinger.'

'What, in the middle of London, in broad daylight?'

'Yes, just that. Can you help us at all?'

'No. I wish I could.'

McLean's gaze went to the piano, on which stood a photograph of Manhattan.

'Have you ever been to the United States?' he asked.

'Yes – years ago.'

'What is your profession?'

'I try out music for a firm of music publishers – not far from here. Hence the piano.'

'May I look round?'

'Certainly. But do you imagine I've got Pullinger locked up in a cupboard?'

The flat was diminutive. There was no room to hide a cat in it. But in the bedroom McLean made an interesting discovery. There was a radiogram close to the bedroom, and standing on top of the gramophone turntable was a single record. It was a very new record, and the title was 'My Mommer' – the music by Harry Pullinger, words by Adele Pullinger.

McLean went back to the sitting-room where Sergeant Brook was still sitting with Trender.

'All right, Brook,' he said. 'We'll get on. Sorry to have troubled you, Mr. Trender.'

'Not at all. Hope you're not going to take my car away.'

'No. Only to look at it.'

III

McLean's examination of the car was cursory. There was the battered mudguard mentioned by the hotel porter, and the number plate as described by the girl in the tobacconist shop. Inside it was clean and tidy.

'There's another man in this,' he said to Brook. 'Trender certainly isn't the man described by the girl. But he lied about not knowing Pullinger. In his bedroom was a gramophone record of Pullinger's latest song hit. I noticed he hadn't a telephone.'

'Where does that come in?' asked Brook.

'It may help us. Drive up the road to a point where we can stop and still see the entrance to this side-street. It is a cul-de-sac, and I think that before very long Mr. Trender may use his car, or one of the public services.'

They waited in the chosen spot for over an hour and still Mr. Trender did not put in an appearance. But McLean was nothing if not patient, and eventually Trender came out from his flat and turned the corner where his car was parked.

'I thought so,' said McLean. 'Get that engine going.'

The subsequent shadowing was a difficult business in the thick traffic, but Brook kept the back of the battered car in sight without approaching close to it, and finally it turned a corner of a street in Chelsea.

'Steady!' said McLean. 'Stop short of the turning, and I'll have a look.'

Brook did this and McLean nipped out of the car, and peered round the corner. He saw Trender leave his car, take a quick look round and then ring the bell at a house. He was let in immediately. McLean got back into the police car, and Brook turned the corner and drove to within fifty yards of the other car. They walked to the house and rang the bell. There was a slight delay and then the door was opened by a tall thin man, with a very obvious stoop.

'I am a police officer,' said McLean. 'What is your name?'

'Hugh Trender.'

'Related to the man who has just arrived here?'

'Yes. He is my brother.'

'Take me to him please.'

The face of the tall man was bloodless. He was breathing hard and clearly overwhelmed. Without a word he led them to a room on the right of the hall. Inside was his brother, and now he too looked terrified. McLean turned to the bent man.

'It was you who drove that car last evening,' he said. 'Don't lie, for I can prove it. Where is Mr. Pullinger?'

Hugh Trender looked at his brother appealingly, and he, unable to speak, pointed to the ceiling.

'Come up!' said McLean, and drove the pair of them into the hall and up the stairs.

The door of a room was opened and inside, lying on a bed, with a sheet over him was Harry Pullinger. There was blood all over his clothing, and a great gash in his head. McLean saw that he had been dead for some time.

'So you killed him!' he said.

'No,' said Albert brokenly. 'We had no intention of harming him. I knew him in the past – in New York. I was composing in those days. I sent him a piece of music of mine, as a hit piece. It had no words. He never returned it and swore it had never reached him. He wasn't married then. When I heard he was to appear in London I went to see the show. It was my music he used for that song "My Mommer" with horrible words by his wife. He had been making a fortune out of my music – passing it off as his own. We – we decided to get him, and hold him until he paid up. Yesterday my brother saw his wife leave the hotel. After getting the car my brother rang up to make sure that Mrs. Pullinger wasn't back. Then he went up to Pullinger's room, and told him that his wife had collapsed outside our house, and had been taken inside. She had asked him to go and tell her husband. He swallowed it all, and was driven here. We told him we wanted a straight deal, but he denied using the music, and said he wouldn't pay a dime. We locked him up for the night, but at one o'clock in the morning he jumped from the window on to the hard paving stones in the yard. He broke a leg and fractured his skull. When we reached him he was dead. That's the whole truth.'

Later a medical report and some evidence in the basement area bore out this statement, but the brothers Trender were destined to be out of circulation for quite a long time, and in certain theatrical quarters there was wailing and gnashing of teeth.

3

OLD Colonel Mountjoy sat down at the large dining table in his lonely house at Hampstead, grumbling at the gout and rheumatics which afflicted him. He grumbled too at having to eat alone, and remembered the days when he and his wife and three children used to keep the place lively with conversation and jokes. Now they had all gone with the exception of the younger son, Richard, who was supposed to live at home, but spent precious little time there.

'Didn't my son say he would be home for dinner?' he asked the maidservant who waited on him.

'He said he wasn't sure, sir,' she replied.

'Dining at his club I suppose,' he grunted. 'Why the devil he should prefer the rotten food they serve there I can't think. That's all, Mary.'

'Shall I serve coffee in your study, sir?'

'No. No coffee, but I'll have a glass of brandy, and to hell with the doctor.'

Later he sat in his study, with his feet up, sipping the brandy and cursing old age and its afflictions, until finally he went to sleep in his chair. It was hours later when he woke up to find his son in the room.

'Hullo, Dick!' he said. 'I thought you were coming home to dinner.'

'Sorry, father, but I got caught up with some friends. You ought to be in bed at this time.'

'So did you,' retorted the Colonel, glancing at the clock. 'It's nearly midnight. I thought the club closed at ten o'clock.'

'It does, but I didn't go to the club. Is there anything I can do for you?'

'No thanks.'

'Then I'll say good night.'

'Good night, my boy!'

The Colonel shook his head as he himself made his way upstairs. He didn't understand Richard – never had. He seemed to be doing fairly well in his job at the War Office, and was usually attentive but he seemed to have no interest at all in the house or the lovely old garden. At twenty-seven he was still single with apparently not the faintest thought of matrimony.

It was on the afternoon of the following day that the Colonel, sitting under his favourite tree in the garden, was informed by Mary that two gentlemen wished to see him, and handed him a card.

'Inspector McLean, of the C.I.D.!' he muttered. 'What the devil can he want? Show him down here.'

McLean and Sergeant Brook soon approached him

from across the lawn, and the Colonel rightly guessed which one was McLean.

'Excuse me from getting up, Inspector,' he said. 'I've a bit of trouble with my foot.'

'That's perfectly all right,' said McLean. 'I'm sorry to trouble you, sir, but are you the owner of a Daimler car, registration number MUO 309?'

'I am,' said the Colonel. 'Why do you ask?'

'Our information is that the car was involved in an incident last night.'

'But that's impossible,' said the Colonel. 'The car wasn't out last night. It hasn't been in use for several days in fact.'

'Can you be sure of that?'

'Quite sure. I have been having a touch of gout, and can't use my right foot properly.'

'Have you a chauffeur?'

'I used to have when I had some money to spend, but not now. There must be some mistake.'

'There could be, of course,' said McLean. 'But the witness seemed quite positive. He said he noticed that the near-side rear light wasn't working.'

'What witness?' asked the Colonel.

'A pedal cyclist who had just been passed by the car, before it knocked down a pedestrian who has since died. I should like to see your car, Colonel.'

'Certainly,' said the Colonel grimly. 'I'll come with you, but I'll be a bit slow.'

He got up and hobbled beside McLean and Brook as he led them to the garage. There he took a key from his pocket and opened the double doors.

'There you are,' he said.

McLean and Brook pushed the Daimler out of the garage into the bright sunshine. Then McLean switched on the lights, and noted that the near-side rear light wasn't working. The Colonel looked down his nose, clearly puzzled.

In the front part of the car McLean found a cigarette stump in the ash-tray, with lipstick on it, and on the floor a small piece of crumpled paper, which bore a rough plan of streets radiating out from a wide irregular space. But it was the rear portion that provided the most important item. On the upholstery of the seat were two dark stains, which looked very much like blood, after some attempt had been made to remove it. McLean drew the Colonel's attention to this.

'I don't understand it,' he said. 'I'm certain it wasn't there when I last used the car some days ago.'

'Was there a woman with you on that occasion?'

'No. There hasn't been a woman in my car in months.'

'And this little drawing – can you throw any light on that?'

'None at all.'

'Is there anyone else in the house who might have used the car yesterday, without your knowledge?'

'No. My son was away from home from about six o'clock until close on midnight.'

'Has he a key to the garage?'

'Yes. He used to run a motor cycle, but he wouldn't have taken my car without asking me.'

'Yet the car was undoubtedly used. When will your son be available?'

'He is usually home about five-thirty. He has a post at the War Office – a civilian job.'

'I'll call back,' said McLean. 'But please don't allow the car to be touched in the meantime.'

II

'You've no doubt that was the car?' asked Brook, when he and McLean were back in their own car.

'None at all, and there's little doubt that an injured person lay on the back seat, and bled there. It looks to me like a double event, in which a man was wounded, and an innocent pedestrian killed. Perhaps it wasn't sheer callousness which induced the driver to go on, but the fear of being questioned about the injured person in the back seat.'

'And a woman seems to be involved.'

'Yes. Until the Colonel's son arrives I want to see what we can make of the rough plan. It may help.'

In his office at Scotland Yard McLean had a large-scale plan of central London, showing all the streets and principal buildings. He and Brook searched diligently for any combination of streets which corresponded with those on the small drawing and at last they found such an area.

27

'Lovelace Gardens!' said Brook. 'Not far from Portland Place.'

'That let's in some light,' said McLean. 'There was an incident in Leyton Terrace reported this morning.'

'That missing witness in the Dodge case?'

'Yes. I think Inspector Drummond has the case. I'll have a word with him.'

Two minutes later McLean was with his colleague.

'Tell me about the Leyton Terrace affair,' he said. 'It may link up with something I have in hand.'

'I wish it did. The missing man is James Hancock, and in two days' time he's wanted at the Old Bailey to give evidence for the Prosecution in the case of Percy Dodge on a charge of manslaughter. On Tuesday, Hancock's wife went to stay with her mother for the night. She returned late yesterday to find her husband not at home. She waited all night, and he never came. Then she came here.'

'How far have you got?'

'Nowhere. There's no sign of any break-in at the house. Nothing to suggest violence. But one can't overlook the significance of Hancock's absence. I'm looking for Dodge's brother, but he's living up to his name. Mrs. Dodge swears she hasn't seen him in weeks, but I know she's lying. Now tell me what's cooking in your mind.'

'It's too early yet,' said McLean. 'A highly respected retired Colonel and his son seem to be involved.'

'What do you mean – involved?'

'I think I've seen the car which was used to remove Hancock from his home. Tell you more when I've checked up any fingerprints which may be on the steering wheel.'

'I thought this was my case,' said Drummond resentfully.

'Only partly. That same car happened to run over a man and kill him. That's my part of it. We'll share the honours later – if there are any.'

'Ever heard about too many cooks spoiling the broth?'

'Stew's a better word. But keep in touch.'

McLean went again to Colonel Mountjoy's house at Hampstead, taking with him Sergeant Brook and two men from the fingerprints department. Richard Mountjoy had not arrived home, but McLean got the garage key from the Colonel and set the fingerprints men to work on the car. A little later the young man came in, and McLean saw him at once – alone.

'Your father's car was involved in an accident last night,' he said. 'He has told me that he himself did not use the car yesterday. Did you use it for any purpose?'

'Yes,' replied Richard, after a brief pause.

'Without informing him?'

'Yes. I needed the car and I came home at shortly after eight o'clock to ask him if I could have it. But I found him dozing in his study, and I didn't like to wake him. As I had a key to the garage I unlocked it and borrowed the car.'

'For what purpose did you use it?'

'A friend of mine wanted to see me urgently.'

'Was it a woman?'

'Yes.'

'What did you do with the car during the time you had it?'

'I took my friend out in it, and drove it back here rather late. A quarter to twelve to be exact.'

'Where was that car at ten-twenty?'

'Parked outside my friend's flat.'

'Mr. Mountjoy – at ten-twenty last night that car ran over a pedestrian at Streatham and killed him.'

The young man's face grew pallid with horror.

'I wasn't in it,' he said. 'I swear I wasn't.'

'I presume your friend will vouch for that. Who is she?'

'I – I don't want to bring her into this,' he replied.

'She must be brought into it, if you want to clear yourself completely. Come, be sensible.'

'But – but she's the wife of my boss. There's nothing in it at all, but he'd never believe it. Don't you realize—?'

'All I realize is that you are behaving stupidly. I want that woman's evidence. It may not go any farther than that.'

'You mean it will not be necessary to tell her husband?'

'He will not know from me.'

'Very well. Her name is Mrs. Delaney, and she lives at Number twenty-six Richmond Terrace, S.W. Her husband is away until tomorrow. She will satisfy you that I was in her company from half-past eight until half-past eleven.'

'Did you leave the car outside her house all that time?'

'No, we drove over to Chelsea and had some drinks there. We returned to the flat about an hour later.'

'When finally you got into your car was it exactly where you had left it?'

'Yes.'

'I suppose that is the truth?' asked Brook, when he and McLean were alone.

'I think so. It's fairly clear that the car was taken by the people who kidnapped Hancock to prevent him giving evidence against Dodge at the Old Bailey, and the fact that the car was back at Richmond Terrace in about an hour after the pedestrian was knocked down suggests that it hadn't far to go after that.'

Later the fingerprint men produced two sets of fingerprints. One lot had been taken from the steering wheel of the car, and were soon proved to be Richard Mountjoy's. The others taken from the inside handle of the rear door were quite different.

'Looks as if a man sat with the injured man, and opened that door as a last act. But who was it?'

Later, as a matter of routine, McLean saw the woman in the case. She corroborated Mountjoy's statement, and McLean had no reason to believe she was not telling the truth.

III

McLean was now in a delicate situation. He did not want to trespass on Drummond's preserve, but could not find the Inspector anywhere to inform him of the position.

'He's evidently out gunning for Dodge's brother, who is careful to keep out of his way. I don't think he'll find Mr. Ignatius Dodge until the trial is over.'

'Is that his name?' asked Brook.

'So I am informed. Brook, have a look at the files. There's just a chance Ignatius may be in them.'

The result of this search was successful, for Ignatius Dodge had served a sentence three years previously for assault and battery.

'Twelve months hard labour,' said McLean, reading the recorded details. 'He was lucky. His confederate got three years – a man named James Kelk. Here are Ignatius's fingerprints. Hand me that one taken from the car door-handle.'

Brook did this and compared the two photographs. There was no resemblance at all.

'Possibly Drummond is barking up the wrong tree,' he mused. 'Let's try Kelk.'

Brook dug out the Kelk records.

'Real thug,' he said. 'Looks capable of murdering his own mother.'

McLean gave a little start as he compared Kelk's fingerprints with the car set.

'Got him!' he said. 'Address at the time of his arrest – Ace of Hearts, South Street, Streatham.'

'I know it,' said Brook. 'It's a cheap café. But I've never been inside the place.'

'Then you shall have the opportunity,' said McLean. 'We shall have to employ a little stealth. Go home and get into an old suit of clothes, and a cap. Go straight to the place and buy yourself something to eat and drink. I'll join you there in a hour and a half. Will that give you time?'

'Plenty.'

'I'll bring a car but will park it some distance away. Be surprised when you see me.'

This plan was carried out to perfection. McLean arrived at the place to find Brook seated not far from the door, looking less like a policeman than McLean had ever seen him, and with a vacant seat opposite. He was eating eggs and bacon as if he enjoyed them. McLean, limping on a heavy stick, with a battered old hat on his head passed through the door.

"ullo Bill!' he said in a rough voice.

Brook stared at him.

'Well I'll be darned!' he said. 'Thought you was in Scotland. Come and sit down. Are you eating?'

'No. Just a cawfee, Bill.'

McLean sat down and gave a glance at the persons present. There were about a dozen customers, all of the working class, two young girls as waitresses, and a grim middle-aged woman behind a counter in charge of the till. One of the girls came forward and McLean ordered a coffee.

'Any sign of our man?' he asked Brook in a low voice.

'No. But the woman behind the counter is Mrs. Kelk. I heard a customer call her that. She took a telephone call just now, and I heard her say, "It's me, Jim. No, he's just gone out for a few minutes. Ten minutes? Okay".'

'Her husband, obviously,' muttered McLean. 'Sounds as if he's on his way here.'

McLean dallied with his coffee, while Brook finished his more substantial repast, and then into the café stepped big Jim Kelk. McLean recognized him at once by his ugly jaw and beetling brow. He took no notice of them but stared at his wife, who shook her head. Then, without a word, he passed through the door which went to the living quarters.

'Do we do anything?' asked Brook.

'Not yet. I want to see the man who went out and hasn't returned.'

'It wasn't long before the expected man arrived. It was Ignatius Dodge – a weakling of a man, with a frightened look. Mrs. Kelk nodded and he went through the door which Kelk had used. The girl came with the bill, and McLean took it.

'I'll settle this,' he said to Brook. 'You go up the road to the right. Fraser has the car there, near the telephone box. Bring it close up. Then come and join me. This may be a rough house before we finish.'

Brook was back in a few minutes, by which time a few of the customers had left, and McLean had paid the bill.

'Okay,' he whispered.

'Then follow me.'

They approached Mrs. Kelk who was now regarding them with, suspicion. McLean said nothing but produced his warrant, and nodded towards the door. Before Mrs. Kelk could recover from the shock they were through the door. A short passage led to a sitting-room, where Kelk and Dodge were seated at a table, drinking whisky.

'What the Hell—!' exclaimed Kelk.

'I am a police officer, and—'

Kelk's hand went to his hip pocket, but before he

could reach it he found himself staring into the steady barrel of an automatic held in McLean's hand.

'Get his gun, Brook!'

Kelk closed with Brook, which was just what Brook wanted. In a matter of seconds Kelk lay on the couch, completely breathless, and with handcuffs on his wrists. McLean turned to the trembling Dodge.

'Where's the man you both kidnapped?' he demanded.

'Out – outside, in the old air-raid shelter,' stammered Dodge.

'And who was driving the car you stole when a man was knocked down and killed?'

Dodge glanced at Kelk, who had now recovered his wits, and Kelk glared back hatefully.

'All right,' said McLean. 'Brook, look after this pair while I'm gone. Yes, you can use that gun.'

McLean went through a door, and finally reached the yard in the rear of the premises. He found steps going down to a well-built old air-raid shelter. Two rough but strong bolts had recently been fitted. He pulled back the bolts, and with the light of a torch saw not one body, but two. One was sitting up, with a bandage round his head. The other was lying, with his face hidden. Both were tightly bound. He went to the sitting man and cut the bonds.

'Are you James Hancock?' he asked.

'Yes. I was assaulted and blindfolded, and thrown in here. They didn't want me to give evidence—'

'I know. I am a police officer. Who is the other man?'

'I don't know. He was brought here an hour ago. I think he is drugged.'

McLean went to the prone man, and pulled his shoulder round. He reeked of chloroform, but was now conscious. McLean stared into a familiar face. It was that of Inspector Drummond!

'You!' gasped Drummond. 'Where am I? I had my hands on that artful Dodge-r, when someone got me from behind. Who's that man?'

'He's your pigeon – the missing star witness. It's wonderful what a bit of co-operation can do, isn't it?'

4

THE case of Lady Batner's necklace made quite a good story. Lady Batner was the wife of Sir Roger Batner, who was on the Board of Directors of a well-known aircraft manufacturing concern, and as a result of the rearmament scheme business was exceptionally good. Lady Batner had always wanted a really first class pearl necklace, and when Sir Roger's company decided to pay a dividend of sixty per cent Lady Batner found her dream come true.

It was as good a pearl necklace as money could buy, and the bill was terrific, but Sir Roger knew that the necklace would put his wife in good humour for months ahead, so the expenditure was well worth while.

'It's lovely, Roger,' she said. 'Now we'll have to give a reception.'

'Not to advertise the necklace?'

'I call that a vulgar remark. Naturally I want people to see it. What about the twenty-fourth?'

Sir Roger looked up his appointments diary, and found that he already had that date booked, so November the twenty-sixth was chosen, and immediately Lady Batner began to make a list of her guests. Invitations were sent to forty people, and in due course some thirty-five of them accepted.

When the great day came Lady Batner was looking her best. She had had a frock made worthy of the necklace, and she felt, and even looked, ten years younger. It was inevitable that her more intimate friends should notice and admire the necklace, and as this was exactly what Lady Batner wanted she was deliriously happy. After the dinner and dancing some special rum punch was served, and it was during this interval that an extraordinary thing happened. Suddenly all the lights went out. A little scream was heard. Someone struck a match, and then the butler came in with two lighted candelabria. Lady Batner was seen clutching her neck, looking quite ill.

'My – my necklace!' she stammered. 'It's – gone.'

Sir Roger hastened to her side, and saw that her plump neck was bare.

'This is amazing,' he said. 'Thomas, what has happened? Have the lights in the hall gone out?'

'No, Sir Roger. I was coming through the hall when I heard a cry. One moment, sir.'

He went to the door and found that the two switches which controlled the two large chandeliers were in the 'off' position. He pushed them down and the lights came on. All the guests were now looking embarrassed, for it was clear that a most bold robbery had been committed.

'What happened, Sarah?' asked Sir Roger. 'Did you feel the necklace snatched?'

'Yes,' she said. 'Just a little tug, nothing more. It was almost immediately after the lights went out. I was standing just where I am now.'

She was about three yards from the switches, with a glass of punch in her hand, which had just been served to her by one of the servants from a big bowl on a table. Sir Roger looked at the guests appealingly.

'There's only one thing to do Roger' said an old friend. 'Get the police here, and I suggest we all stay where we are until they arrive.'

'Oh, no, I can't do that. You are all my—'

'Cantler's right,' said another man. 'You must get the police.'

'Well, at least let us look round. It may have been a coincidence,' said Sir Roger.

'Switches don't go up by coincidence. Don't waste any time.'

There was a low buzz of conversation while Sir Roger made up his unwilling mind. Finally he rang up the police, as a result of which Inspector McLean and Sergeant Brook arrived at the house about a quarter of an hour later. Sir Roger explained the situation privately.

'Every one of the guests is well-known to me,' he said. 'Yet it is a fact that the necklace was deliberately snatched from my wife's neck.'

'Where were the servants?' asked McLean.

'The butler was between the drawing-room and the kitchen, and the footman was serving drinks. There was also a girl – Nellie – helping him.'

'Was the door into the hall shut tightly at the time?'

'I think so.'

35

'The necklace I presume is of some value?'

'It cost me over five thousand pounds – six weeks ago.'

'Has anyone left the drawing-room since this happened?' asked McLean.

'No. I requested them all to stay until you arrived.'

'Good! I had better go to the drawing-room.'

Sir Roger accompanied him and Brook to the large room, where the guests were still in a state of tremendous excitement. McLean was introduced and became the focus of every eye.

'Ladies and gentlemen,' he said. 'It might help if you would all be good enough to occupy the positions you held when the lights went out.'

There were many movements on the part of the gathering. The footman stayed where he was standing over the big bowl of rum punch, of which very little now remained. The very attractive maid was at the back of the room near the fireplace. Lady Batner was a few steps from the door with her back to it, and her husband to her left also with his back to the door.

'Thank you,' said McLean. 'Can any lady or gentleman remember whether the door was completely shut?'

One man said he had left the room a few minutes before and had come back to it, closing the door behind him. But another said he felt sure the door had been slightly open, and this rather bore out the butler's statement that he had heard Lady Batner's cry, and had come to the door in response to a call from a gentleman.

'Who was it who called?' asked McLean.

A man named Crowe, who was near the door, inclined his head.

'I did,' he said. 'But I'm blest if I can remember whether the door was properly shut. Someone struck a match and I saw the brass handle, and opened the door. I was so excited I can't swear that the door wasn't properly shut. I saw the butler at the end of the hall – coming from the kitchen I think.'

'That's correct,' said the butler.

McLean examined the two switches which were of the up and down type, and side by side, to see if they could have been accidentally operated by someone pressing backwards against them. But this was not credible. He then examined the chairs and settees in the room, and investigated two large pots which held flowers, while the guests followed every movement.

It was Cantler who made a bold suggestion.

'Roger,' he said. 'We're all friends of each other, and I think we should all feel relieved if the officers would carry out a personal search. After all, it's a definite theft and not merely a loss.'

The men murmured their approval, but the ladies weren't quite so eager. Still, there was no objection from anyone.

McLean looked at Sir Roger.

'It would be unforgivable,' protested Sir Roger.

'Rubbish!' replied Cantler. 'I'm certain it will help the Inspector enormously· Isn't that so, Inspector?'

'Yes,' replied McLean. 'I won't deny that.'

'Then please make a start on me,' said Cantler.

There was a laugh, and the awkward stage was surmounted. One by one the guests came forward, and were quickly eliminated. The first lady looked a little embarrassed, but after a few minutes it was looked upon as great fun. Handbags were opened, and hair examined. The two servants came last, and were found to be as innocent as the guests.

'Hurrah!' said Cantler. 'Everyone with a clean sheet.'

McLean then suggested that the guests should go to another room for a short time, as he would like to make a closer examination of the drawing-room. They all filed out, talking breathlessly.

II

'Is this some sort of a game?' grumbled Brook. 'The blessed thing couldn't evaporate.'

'It may have been hidden,' said McLean. 'Take those cushions out of the chairs and the settee, and look inside the piano.'

Inch by inch the large room was scrutinized. Even the chimney was suspect, but it yielded nothing. McLean then opened the two large windows, and shone a torch into the garden outside. The windows were so stiff he didn't think they could have been opened, and in addition the cold air outside was immediately noticeable after the very hot room.

'Sir Roger said no one left the room,' he mused. 'But he left himself – to come to us.'

'Good Lord! You don't think—'

'Oh no, but it's a thing to remember. Personally I'm inclined to think it was done from outside. If the door was ajar it wouldn't be very difficult. Let us see.'

He opened the door slightly, and placed Brook where Lady Batner had been standing. Then he went outside, and with the door a few inches open he put his hand round and in one swift movement pressed both switches upwards. The lights went out. Brook felt a touch on his face and in a moment the lights were up and he was alone in the room. The door was not quite closed. McLean came to view.

'The light in the hall is well away from this door,' he said. 'With the room in darkness anyone could enter and not be seen. We'd better look into the matter of servants. Ring that bell.'

The bell brought the butler in. He said that just before the lights went out he went into the kitchen. It was on coming back into the main hall that he heard Lady Batner's cry from the drawing-room. As he approached the door it was opened and he heard that the lights had failed. He quickly lighted two candelabras and took them into the room.

'Did you see anyone in the hall as you came round the corner from the domestic part of the house?' asked McLean.

'No one, sir.'

'What other servants are there in the house apart from the footman, and the girl Nellie?'

'There is Alphonse – the French Chef, an under-footman, who was in charge of the cloak-room, and two other maids.'

'Which of these were in the kitchen, when you went there?'

'Alphonse and Dora. I didn't see Ethel, the parlour-maid, but thought she was in the servants hall.'

'Where was the under-footman?'

'In the cloak-room, reading.'

'You didn't see him on your way to the drawing-room?'

'Oh no. It was just afterwards that I saw him there.

38

'How long have these various servants been in Sir Roger's employ?'

'Alphonse has been here as long as I have – four years. The others are all very recent. It's a terrible job to keep servants these days.'

'I think we will have them all in here.'

'You mean all at once?'

'Yes, except the footman and Nellie.'

The butler went out and a few minutes later he came back with the other two women, Alphonse, and the under-footman. Alphonse was alibi for Dora, and vice versa. Neither of them had left the kitchen for at least a quarter of an hour before the robbery was committed. Lake, the under-footman, swore that he had never left the cloak-room since he had been stationed there. He was an honest enough looking man, but McLean had to remember that he had no alibi and could possibly have got to the door of the drawing-room.

Ethel Mayne also had to be taken at her word. She was a dreamy kind of girl, and had only come to the house a few weeks before. She said she had had a lot of work to do and that the footman told her she could rest that evening. She had taken a seat by the fire in the servant's hall, and had been busy knitting herself a jumper.

The problem seemed no nearer a solution. It was reasonable to rule out Alphonse and Dora, because to bring them under suspicion would involve the butler, and McLean couldn't believe that there had been three persons in the plot. Since the footman and Nellie had been in the room when the robbery had taken place, and had been searched it was difficult to see how they could have had any hand in the matter. Only Lake and Ethel were thus left. McLean dismissed them all, and then went to another room, in order to allow the guests to return. Sir Roger came to him.

'Any progress, Inspector?' he asked.

'Very little so far. I propose to search the rest of the house. Are all the servants satisfactory?'

'I've no reason to doubt any of them, but of course only two of them have been with me for any length of time – the butler and Alphonse. I'm absolutely certain they are the soul of honesty.'

'In that case Dora is also innocent, for Alphonse says she was with him, and the butler endorses that.'

'Oh yes, she's a very nice girl.'

'What about the new parlourmaid?'

'From what I've seen of her I should think she's straight enough. As a matter of fact I dropped a five-pound note a week ago. I should never have missed it because it was one of a bundle, but she found it in my bedroom and gave it to me.'

'And the under-footman?'

'He's rather a clod. I can't imagine Lake having the skill to steal an umbrella.'

'That seems to exonerate absolutely everyone,' said McLean, with a smile, 'Yet the necklace has gone.'

'I know. It's quite bewildering – baffling.'

He went back to his guests, and McLean and Brook started a search of the house. It was a thankless task in view of the size of the place, but experience had taught them where not to look, and the job was done with considerable care.

'The trouble is the possibility of some outside person being involved,' said McLean. 'There was time to slip the necklace. If that has taken place our chances are pretty small. What's this room?'

'Servant's hall,' said Brook.

They knocked and went in. The girl – Ethel – was sitting by a nice log fire knitting.

'Oh!' she exclaimed.

'Sorry to disturb you,' said McLean. 'But it's necessary to search the whole house.'

'That's all right,' she said. 'I do hope you find it.'

But her hopes were vain. For two solid hours McLean and Brook spent their time searching in drawers, under carpets, between mattresses, everywhere where there was space enough to hide the necklace temporarily. It was past midnight when they finally came downstairs, and saw Sir Roger.

'No luck,' said McLean.

'Could it have been got out of the house?'

'That's possible.'

'What am I to do? I mean I can't very well detain any of my guests.'

'Certainly not. I should like you to give me a complete

list of them, with their addresses, and it's most necessary that no servant leaves the house without permission. I need to look up the servants' histories, so I shall want the names of their last employers.'

'Thomas can give you that. We are most careful about references.'

The butler supplied McLean with all the details in his possession, and Sir Roger added to this a list of his guests. But when he finally left he told Brook to stay near the house.

'There may be an attempt to get the necklace out, after the guests have gone,' he said. 'That is if it isn't out already. Keep a close watch on things.'

'All night?' asked Brook.

'I'll arrange for a man to relieve you at two o'clock. If any of the servants attempt to leave stop them. If you see anyone loitering take him in charge.'

III

The next morning McLean heard that Brook had been relieved as arranged. The last guest left at a quarter past one, and by two o'clock the house was in darkness. The man who had relieved Brook had telephoned to say that no one had left the house. McLean instructed him to stay on until he himself arrived.

It was a long time before this could take place, as he had a number of inquiries to make. Lake's history was quite satisfactory. He had been in domestic service all his life, and there was nothing against him, except his slowness and general lack of intelligence.

'He couldn't have undertaken that job,' said McLean. 'It was a very slick affair, and called for courage and agility.'

Ethel had been a little more difficult to investigate. She had not come through an agency but in reply to an advertisement in a newspaper. References had been supplied by her late employer, and as the woman was in London McLean went to see her. She made no accusation of dishonesty, but she said that the girl was a mysterious character. She knew that she was in the habit of dining at quite expensive restaurants with men – or a man. Her last employer had discharged her because

of her late habits. McLean went to see the previous
employer. She also was uncertain about Ethel. She herself
had lost a rather valuable brooch, and had never
recovered it. She said she was sure she hadn't lost the
brooch outside the house, and her other servants were
undoubtedly trustworthy, but she had no evidence to
show that Ethel was the guilty person, and so she dared
not do otherwise than give the girl a reference. McLean
went one more step backwards. This time it was a very
large establishment in the home counties. Ethel had been
employed there for six months as parlourmaid. The story
was much the same. Some jewellery had been missing.
But the real reason why the girl was sacked was that she
was found in the bedroom of the footman late at night.

'It was true,' said the lady, 'That Tice found an
excuse—'

'Tice,' interrupted McLean. 'Was that the footman's
name?'

'Yes. Robert Tice. 'He left soon after the girl, because
he thought he had been placed in an embarrassing
position.'

'Thank you,' said McLean.

'Looks like a bad character,' said Brook. 'But even so
I can't think she did this job?'

'Why not?'

'Because the whole thing was very difficult.'

'Not for two persons,' said McLean.

'You mean outside help?'

'I do not. You've got a terrible memory for names.
Doesn't Tice mean anything to you?'

'No.'

'He's on our list. He's footman to Sir Roger.'

McLean showed him the list of names which the butler
had given him. Brook whistled his surprise.

'But he was in the room. We searched him,' he said.

'We did, and found nothing. We didn't suspect him
because he was working when the lights went out, but
with an accomplice outside the thing was easy.'

'You mean the girl did the light trick?'

'Isn't that the obvious solution? All she had to do was
put a hand round the door and switch off the lights.
Then hurry back to the servants hall, and go on with her
knitting.'

'But do you mean that Tice pinched the necklace?'

'You saw the position of the persons in the room. Lady Batner was quite close to Tice. He had only to move a step to reach her and snatch the necklace. It would account for the fact that no one saw anyone enter the room. I agree it was quite dark when the room lights went out, but even so an intruder had to get in, and out again, in a few moments, because someone struck a match almost at once.'

'But we searched him,' repeated Brook.

'That's true. But I'm certain that those two are responsible. Remember that they were in service together, and on very familiar terms. Then the girl comes to Sir Roger just after his wife had been given a very valuable necklace. She wasn't working last night. She said the footman told her she could rest. Tice didn't want her to work. He wanted her to be on hand for the carrying out of the job. There may have been a signal arranged. He could have dropped a heavy ladle on the parquet floor. She would hear it if she were listening. Anyway, lets see how things work out.'

They drove to the house, and stopped near it to talk to the watching detective. He said that no one had left the house, except Sir Roger. McLean dismissed him and rang the bell. He was let in by Tice.

'Oh, Mr. Tice,' said McLean. 'I should like to ask you a few questions.'

'Certainly Inspector,' replied Tice. 'The morning room is vacant.'

'That will do.'

They went to the morning room. Tice looked quite calm, as he waited for the questions.

'I believe Miss Mayne was the last girl to come here,' said McLean.

'That's true.'

'Who engaged her?'

'The butler.'

'What do you think of her personally?'

'She strikes me as being a very good girl – clean with her work and always willing and polite.'

'Do you think she may have a man friend?'

'I really don't know.'

'Do you know anything about her past?'

'Why, no. She doesn't gossip much, and of course she has only been here a few weeks.'

'But you have had other opportunities,' said McLean. 'You were in service with her at Lady Leets, weren't you?'

Tice couldn't cover up his surprise, but he was quick to explain matters.

'That's true,' he said. 'She was the victim of a misunderstanding, and that is why I didn't mention that I had already met her.'

'Did you take steps to help her get this post?'

'Oh no. It was quite a coincidence.'

'I'm sorry I don't believe you, Mr. Tice,' said McLean. 'That's all at the moment.'

Tice went out, and Brook chuckled when the door closed after him.

'That caught him,' he said. 'He's now as nervous as a cat on hot bricks. But what did he do with the necklace?'

'I've an idea,' said McLean. 'It may be quite wrong, but it would explain everything. Come into the kitchen.'

They entered the kitchen where Alphonse and a daily girl were busy. The chef didn't like being disturbed when he was preparing lunch, and let the fact be known.

'Listen,' said McLean. 'You remember Mr. Tice taking in the rum punch last night?'

'Yes, M'sieur.'

'Were you here when he came out with the bowl, after we had questioned him?'

'Yes. But I go to talk with Dora about the robbery and leave him here.'

'Did you see what he did with the remainder of the punch?'

'No. He say it was very good, and that the pigs they drink it all.'

'That wasn't true,' said McLean. 'There was a quantity left.'

'Maybe he pour the dregs away.'

'I think you're right,' said McLean.

He went to the large sink, and took a look at the drain plug. It was a very large one, and under it was a perforated piece of copper, which came out easily. McLean turned on the tap, and the water ran away freely. He then bent down and saw the S bend in the

44

large drain pipe. A thumbscrew nut at the bottom was there for the purpose of dealing with any obstruction. McLean removed the nut and some dirty water ran out into a pail which he pushed underneath. He put his little finger inside the orifice, and felt something. A few more attempts and out came the pearl necklace, looking very second-hand.

'*Mon Dieu!*' ejaculated Alphonse.

As McLean expected, Tice denied all knowledge of the necklace, he admitted pouring what was left of the punch down the sink, because it was very thick. Perhaps some-one had dropped the necklace into it.

'Someone did,' said McLean. 'Someone also had to lift up the piece of perforated copper in order to make room for the necklace to pass. That person was you, Mr. Tice. You and Miss Mayne are under arrest. By the way, I shouldn't be surprised if Miss Mayne's real name is Mrs. Tice.'

Later investigations proved McLean to be correct.

5

GALTON HOUSE in Essex was a curious place from many points of view. It was a rambling, half-timbered place, with a very large and wild garden abutting on a small river, which was navigable all the way to the sea at anything but low tide. It lay off any main road and was five miles from the nearest town. From the point of view of the antiquarian there was much that was interesting in the house for the earlier part of it was fifteenth-century, but it had been allowed to get into a sad state of disrepair, and as a residence it was now far from pleasant, for there were rats in the walls, and no proper sanitation. In addition the only form of lighting was a gas plant.

The present owner – James Bogley – was, according to common gossip, as strange as the house. He was on very bad terms with his family and rather than suffer their company he had built himself a wooden bungalow at the far end of the garden, and in this shanty he spent most of his life.

On the morning of November the first his dead body was found by the maidservant who brought him his breakfast, and later the same day McLean and Sergeant Brook motored down from London to investigate the case.

They arrived at Galton late in the afternoon, in a fog which had been increasing all day. McLean had had instructions to go direct to the bungalow, and he found there a young officer of the local police trying vainly to keep himself warm, for there was no heating but a paraffin stove.

'I'm Detective Maldon, sir,' he said. 'Superintendent Young told me you were coming. He was called away.'

'I saw him at headquarters,' said McLean. 'But I understood Doctor Benrook was here.'

'He had to leave on an urgent case. He told me to tell you he would return as soon as possible.'

McLean nodded and took a look round the place. It was diminutive and comprised but two rooms, the larger of which was the sitting-room. This contained a large table, a settee, two easy chairs, and several bookcases, full of books. On the floor were several very old rugs. The lighting was provided by a hanging oil lamp.

The inner room was a bedroom, and contained nothing but the small bed, a table and a cane chair. The bed was now made, and the room tidy. McLean came back to the sitting-room, and removed a blanket from the face of the corpse, which was occupying the settee. He was a man of about forty-five with short brown beard and moustache. The head was large, and the features small and regular. In the breast were two bullet wounds. The doctor arrived as McLean was replacing the blanket, and was introduced by the detective.

'Sorry I had to leave for a short while,' he said. 'I had to give an injection. You've taken a look at him?'

He glanced towards the settee, and McLean nodded.

'There's not much to say,' he said. 'I was called here at eight o'clock this morning. I found Mr. Bogley lying on the floor – his feet towards the door, and his back against the settee. I've chalked the position of the feet. He was dead, and had obviously been dead for some time. I made tests during the day, and my conclusion is that he died from the two wounds at some time during

46

the night. I should put the time at between one and two
o'clock.'

'Can you say how long he would survive the wounds?'

'That's a difficult question. It might have been an hour,
and it might have been less. I should give an hour as the
maximum time.'

'So there is really a time margin of two hours? At the
earliest he might have been shot at midnight, and died
at one o'clock.'

'That's true.'

'And it's possible that he was shot just before two
o'clock?'

'Yes – if he died almost immediately. I don't think he
could have died as quickly as that, because of the quantity of blood on the rug.'

'Which rug?'

'I had to put it outside. I'll show you.'

He conducted McLean outside and showed him a fairly
large rug which was hanging on a bush, and was in sorry
condition. They came back to the bungalow.

'Were you his regular medical attendant?' asked
McLean.

'Yes, but he was seldom ill. For a man of his habits he
kept remarkably fit.'

'What habits?'

'He was a heavy drinker, and took scarcely any exer-
cise. I know that he thought nothing of sitting up night
after night reading and drinking.'

'Did he read for pleasure or profit?'

'Profit. He was a literary man, and wrote, I think, on
sociology.'

'Was that his sole means of livelihood?'

'I really don't know. I did hear that his wife is a very
wealthy woman, but that may only be gossip.'

'Did he live here all the time?'

'For the past five years. His meals are brought to him
from the house. Apparently he quarrelled with his wife
and sons, and went away for a time, but he came back
after a year, and started to live apart from the family.'

'Has he ever indicated the cause of the quarrel?'

'No. He was far too proud a man to do that.'

'Do you attend his wife?'

'No. I've never even met her.'

The doctor left soon after, and McLean was able to examine the bungalow in greater detail. In a cupboard he found a large quantity of drink, and a number of glasses, and in an old desk he found a number of small manuscripts, all apparently dealing with the subject of sociology. Documents showed that the dead man had an Oxford degree. All the volumes in the bookcases were serious works, and had been much read. There were a number of quite recent publications – some in foreign languages.

On the table were two empty cartridge cases which had been picked up by the local police, and near them were articles taken from the clothing of the dead man. The articles were of no interest, but McLean looked closely at the cartridge cases, and then took from a box in his pocket the two bullets which had been given him at police headquarters.

'An American automatic,' he said. 'Looks like a Colt.'

'It's a Colt all right,' agreed Brook.

Despite the amount of blood on the rug outside there was no trace of it on the floor.

'It looks as if the murderer just came inside the door, and shot from that position,' said McLean. 'There's no sign of any disturbance. Maldon, was that book on the table when you arrived?'

'Yes, Inspector.'

'And that chair – have you shifted it?'

'No. I was told not to move a thing.'

McLean took the book and opened it. It was *Das Kapitol* by Karl Marx.

'It looks as if he was reading, in that chair, and rose when he was interrupted,' mused McLean.

He examined the hanging oil lamp and found the reservoir quite empty. Clearly it had burnt out during the night.

'I'll take some evidence before we go any further,' he said to Brook.

'If you want to ring the house there's a telephone here,' said Maldon. 'Under that cover.'

He pointed to a doll, the skirt of which covered a telephone receiver. McLean lifted the receiver, and found that he was on to the exchange. The operator told him to switch over to the house, and this he did on a small

dial close to the receiver. He then asked Mrs. Bogley to
be good enough to come to the bungalow.

II

Mrs. Bogley was a handsome woman of about forty
years of age. Her eyes were now a little swollen from
weeping, a fact which she had obviously done her best to
eradicate without success. McLean had pushed the settee
round so that its grim burden was invisible to her.

'Please sit down,' he said. 'I am Inspector McLean of
Scotland Yard, and I wish to ask you a few questions
relative to this matter.'

Mrs. Bogley occupied the chair, and sat facing McLean,
while Brook took shorthand notes.

'When did you last see your husband alive?' asked
McLean.

'Yesterday morning. I saw him walk across to the house
to wash.'

'Did he always use the house for that purpose?'

'Yes.'

'Did you speak to him?'

'No.'

'Were you not on speaking terms with him?'

'Oh yes, but we didn't often speak.'

'So you were estranged?'

'Yes.'

'Does that apply to his two sons?'

'No. He and the younger boy got on very well, but
Harry, the elder boy has never got on with him.'

'Where are the two sons?'

'The younger one is still at school, but Harry is at
home. He finished school in the summer, and is soon to
go into business.'

'Was there any definite cause for this disharmony?'

'He was a difficult man. He treated us so contemptu-
ously – disliked us because we didn't share his views on
politics and religion. Years ago he left me, but he came
back again, because he found he couldn't work away
from here.'

'Did he live by his writing?'

'Yes – personally. But I have had the expense of bringing up the boys and in running the house. I didn't

49

complain about that, because I knew he was poor when I married him.'

'Did he go to the house for meals?'

'Yes.'

'At what time was he last seen there?'

'At eight o'clock last night. The maidservant served his meal at seven o'clock in the morning room. I should mention that his breakfast was always brought here.'

'Can you throw any light at all on this matter?'

'No.'

'When did you learn about it?'

'This morning at eight o'clock. I was dressing when the maid came and told me.'

'And the son – where was he last night?'

'Harry was indoors reading until eleven o'clock. He then went to bed, and I went a few minutes later.'

The son was then called. He was a tall boy and said that his age was eighteen. He stated that he went to bed at eleven o'clock the previous night, and was awakened soon after eight that morning by his mother who told him the bad news. He had last seen his father at lunch time the previous day when he came over for a meal.

'Why did you take such a dislike for your father?' asked McLean.

'I didn't until a few years ago, when I was old enough to realize that he was the cause of my mother's unhappiness.'

'In what way?'

'He treated her like an inferior despite the fact that he was living on her money, and that it was she who paid for our education – everything in fact.'

'Your mother has private money?'

'Oh yes. She inherited a large fortune when her father died ten years ago.'

'Has your brother been sent for?'

'Yes. He is due home at any moment.'

'I wish to see him the moment he arrives. Have you ever seen a firearm of any sort in the house?'

'Only a shot-gun.'

'Can you think of any reason why anyone should kill your father?'

'No – none at all.'

'Didn't you at any time last night notice the light burning here?'

'No. You can't see this place from any room in the house, and I never went out after dinner.'

'What servants are there in the house?'

'Two. A maidservant and cook, but cook doesn't sleep in.'

'Please tell the maidservant I wish to speak to her.'

The girl entered the bungalow a few minutes later. She too had been crying, but she answered up well. She said she had been with the family for three years, and during all that time the 'master' had lived apart from his wife and sons. She admitted he was difficult to get on with, but he had always treated her well.

'Have you ever heard a quarrel?'

'Oh no. He wasn't quarrelsome. If he was annoyed he would only show it by his expression.'

'When the elder son was at school Mrs. Bogley was left alone wasn't she?'

'Oh yes, in term time.'

'Did she go out much?'

'Not a great deal, perhaps once a week she would go to London. You see, we haven't any near neighbours. Mrs. Bogley is a very good pianist, and she loves to stay in and play the piano.'

'Last night when Mr. Bogley came into the house for his dinner – was he quite normal – I mean quite his usual self?'

'Oh yes. He made a good meal, and told me it was a very nice dinner.'

At this juncture the younger son knocked on the door, and McLean dismissed the girl. The boy was very like his brother, but several years younger. He was evidently suffering from shock, for he appeared to be dazed. McLean had difficulty in getting him to concentrate on the matter at hand. He said his name was Ralph, and that he hadn't seen his father since he went back to school for the autumn term. But he had heard from his father several times. Questioned about the family disharmony he gave it as his opinion that it wasn't all the fault of his father.

'Mother never quite realized the type of man father was,' he said. 'I mean she never really tried to get herself interested in his outlook. Father was a dreamer – always in the clouds, looking for a better world. That was why he drank so heavily – to escape from things as they are. Years ago I used to think he was harsh and unsympathetic, but lately I've been able to understand him. At heart he was very kind. He wanted friendship and love, and yet always gave people the impression that he had no emotions. Perhaps you've met that sort of man, sir?'

'I have,' said McLean with a smile. 'Now did your father ever give you the slightest cause to suspect that he might have an enemy?'

'Oh no.'

'Have you at any time seen a pistol in the house?'

'Never.'

'And you're not able to throw any light at all on this tragedy?'

The boy's eyes filled with tears, and he shook his head. McLean told him he had no more questions to ask at the moment, and the boy left the bungalow. A little later the body was removed, and McLean and Brook were left alone to make what they could of the strange business. Everything in the bungalow was now most carefully examined. Relevant documents were collected together, and placed on the table. According to a recent bank statement the dead man had the sum of fifty pounds in the bank. There were two share certificates, for a hundred shares each in second-rate companies. A paying-in book showed that he paid into the bank sums of money ranging from three to ten guineas at fairly regular intervals, and a record book showed where and when he had sold literary material. Some of his articles were pasted up in a paper-cuttings book. They were all very abstruse.

'No wonder Mrs. Bogley got a bit bored,' said Brook, as he scanned some of these. 'A bit Communistic, wasn't he?'

McLean nodded, as he turned over the pages of a neatly written diary. It was a beautiful piece of literature, and was evidently intended to be private. It covered a period of four years, and was up to date for the last entry had been made but two days before. In this very intimate book James Bogley made himself as clear as crystal. But there was nothing in it which seemed to throw any light on the murder.

'Just a man looking at himself critically and fearlessly,' said McLean. 'There's no hate here against any person, so far as I can see. He know's he is difficult to understand, and is hurt by his wife's increasing coldness, and that of his elder son. He believes they regard him as a failure, and wonders if in a sense they aren't right, since he finds love and friendship so difficult to win. H'm, I'll take this to bed with me.'

Searching the garden in the fog and damp was no pleasant task. There was little hope of finding footprints, as there was a gravel path leading from the main drive through the shrubberies to the bungalow, and finally McLean had to give it up. But it was clear that the pistol used was not in the immediate vicinity of the bungalow.

'We'll look over the house, and then finish for tonight,' he said. 'If the fog goes before morning we'll make an early start.'

Mrs. Bogley appreciated the need for searching the house, since some of her husband's effects were still in the bedroom he used to occupy. She showed him the room, and told him that the rest of the house was at his disposal.

The bedroom yielded nothing of any value, for its contents were restricted to articles of clothing, and the normal furniture. McLean went into the next room, which was obviously Mrs. Bogley's. It was much better furnished than the rest of the house, and showed her to be a woman who loved rather exotic things. McLean found nothing here but two letters from a man who signed himself 'Joe'. He took the address of the writer. The rooms of the two boys were very bare, and took only a few minutes of his time. At the end of the passage he found the maid's room. She had evidently just gone out, for there were signs of a rapid change of clothing. Here there wasn't much to engage McLean's attention, and after looking through the chest of drawers, and through a large tin trunk, he went downstairs. The cook was in the kitchen preparing an evening meal. McLean asked her a few questions, and soon came to the conclusion that she wouldn't be helpful, for she was quite antagonistic.

'I know nothing at all,' she said. 'At seven o'clock each evening I 'op it. I've only been here a year, and I haven't spoken to Mr. Bogley twice during that time. That suited me all right. If there's been a murder committed I'm not getting myself mixed up in it. My job is to cook, and that's all I'm interested in.'

'I wish all cooks could say the same,' sighed McLean.

He and Brook went to the neighbouring town a little later and found accommodation.

III

Somewhat unexpectedly the morning dawned clear and bright, and McLean had Brook out of bed actually before sunrise.

'I've ordered breakfast at once,' he said. 'I want to get back on the job.'

Breakfast was a smash and grab affair, and they were soon on the road. By the time they reached Galton House the sun had risen and was transforming the countryside. Galton House looked very different in the refulgent light. The large and very overgrown garden looked much less sinister, and even the house was less grim. Some work was being done on flower beds, near the house, and McLean was pleased that at least some attempt was being made to save the place from becoming a complete wilderness.

He had the key of the bungalow and let himself in, but as he opened the door he stopped and peered through the blades of a scraper which was outside the door. Wedged between the bars was something. He picked it out with a match and saw that it was a piece of chewing-gum. It's condition caused him to believe it had been discarded recently.

'I can't quite imagine Bogley chewing such filth,' he said. 'Yet somebody left it.'

After disposing of their overcoats and hats they went out into the garden again, and continued their search, but found nothing. McLean inspected the flower beds under the wall, and the bank of the creek close to the garden, but nowhere was there a single sign of a footprint. Then a man arrived on a cycle, and rode close to a potting shed where he dismounted, and took his cycle inside. In a few minutes he emerged with a spade, minus his coat. McLean went across to him.

'Are you the gardener?' he asked.

54

'In a way, sir. But I only come here three days a week. It's a pity because the garden is going back to nature.'

'How long have you been employed here?'

'Four years, but never whole time. I wish I had been, but Mrs. Bogley wouldn't hear of it.'

'What is your name?'

'Charles Boon, sir.'

'I presume you know there has been a crime committed here?'

'Yes, sir. Everybody knows that. Poor Mr. Bogley! He was such a quiet man, too.'

McLean turned away, and Boon walked towards a flower bed, which was in process of being dug up.

'Must have been in the war,' mused McLean. 'Yet he doesn't look old enough for that.'

'Why do you think he was in the war?' asked Brook.

'Didn't you see that scar in his wrist? It was a bullet wound.'

'But he doesn't look more than thirty.'

'Must be nearly forty. I read Bogley's diary last night in bed. A meritorious piece of work. Interesting if one reads between the lines.'

'How do you mean?'

'A love-starved man finding relief unexpectedly.'

'Where?'

'Ah, that's the problem. I'm going to the bungalow. I want you to go to the house and bring Alice, the servant, across.'

Brook arrived at the bungalow a few minutes after McLean, with the pretty maidservant.

'Sit down Alice,' said McLean quietly.

The girl did so, and stared at him fixedly.

'How long have you been in love with Boon?' he asked.

The girl gave an involuntary start.

'I'm not,' she protested. 'I hate him.'

'Yet you keep his photograph in your room – even though it was face downwards in the tin trunk.'

'Oh,' she gasped. 'That – that's all over – now.'

'So you did fall in love with him?'

'Yes.'

'Why did you break it off?'

'He accused me of flirting. He threatened to – to do something to me if I didn't stop. He was so rude I told him I'd never go out with him again, and I haven't spoken to him since.'

'When was this?'

'A week ago, when he took me to a cinema. He was quiet all the evening, and when bringing me home he started on me.'

'And was there any truth in his accusations?'

'No – none at all.'

McLean looked at her sternly, and she seemed to wilt before his gaze.

'Are you sure, Alice?'

'Why – yes,' she stammered.

'Mr. Bogley was quite kind to you, wasn't he?'

'Oh yes.'

'You used to wait on him at the house. In addition you used to bring his breakfast here every morning, at about eight o'clock?'

'Yes,' she quavered.

'Did Mr. Bogley ever show his appreciation in any way?'

'Well, he has given me some boxes of chocolates – at times.'

'But did he ever tell you he liked you? Has he ever kissed you when you came here?'

The girl's face went crimson, she was about to deny this, but somehow McLean's intent gaze prevented it.

'He – he did kiss me – once or twice,' she stammered. 'I didn't think there was any harm in that – him living all alone, and Mrs. Bogley not caring what happened to him. If you think that anything else happened you're wrong—'

'I don't think anything of the sort. Dry your eyes and go back to your work.'

'Phew!' said Brook. 'Now we're getting somewhere.'

'I think so. You see, Alice brought the breakfast across about the same time that Boon started work. I think we shall find he was a very observant man. I want to have a look inside his coat.'

This was done a little later, when Boon was working out of sight of the potting shed. The coat provided half a packet of well-known chewing gum. McLean had the stuff analysed that afternoon, and it was proved to be the same as the lump he had found. But this in itself was no proof of murder. The next step was a visit to Boon's cottage. Boon was out at work, but a woman was there tidying up for him. She stated that she came in every morning for an hour.

'Have you ever seen a pistol here?' asked McLean.

'Why yes. It's in the sitting-room on the wall. Mr. Boon brought it back from France after the war. I'll show you.'

She took McLean into the sitting-room. On the mantelpiece were two polished brass shell cases, and in the fender a poker made from a German bayonet. But the pistol wasn't in its usual place.

'When did you last see it?' asked McLean.

'Within the last few days. Perhaps two days ago.'

An hour later Boon was arrested. He denied ever having a pistol and said that the charwoman must have been lying. But several neighbours were found who had seen the pistol, and one of them was able to give the make. It wasn't a Colt as McLean believed the guilty pistol to be, but the firearms expert pointed out that the two pistols were almost identical, and that anyone might make the same mistake. Then, two days later, the pistol was found in a pond on the road between Galton House and Boon's cottage. It was identified by several persons.

Later Boon confessed. He said he had seen the girl in Bogley's arms on two occasions, and in a fit of mad rage, after the girl had jilted him he went and killed the man responsible. Medical evidence was put in to show that Boon had suffered from brain storms as a result of shell-shock in the war. A merciful verdict was returned.

'Bogley himself gave me the clue,' said McLean. 'That diary of his is a great piece of work. I salute him, for the skill with which he showed the workings of a man's troubled soul.'

6

PRIOR to her trip to sunny Madeira old Lady Wimster did what she always did on that annual occasion. She boxed up all her silver and such jewellery as she would not require on her holiday, locked the steel box, retained the key, and sent her maid with the box to her bank, where a receipt was issued, marked 'Locked, and unexamined.'

'You cannot be too careful, Emma,' she said. 'Burglars are so enterprising these days.'

Nor was this her only precaution. She went to the small local police station, slipped a pound note into the hand of Sergeant Kent, whom she knew well, and informed him that she would be away for six weeks, and asked him to keep an eye on her house.

'I'll do that, my lady,' he said.

'The gardener will be coming on Mondays, Wednesdays and Fridays as usual, but there will be no one in the house, as my housekeeper will be with her people in Scotland.'

'Very good, my lady.'

After giving her temporary change of address to the Post Office, Lady Wimster and her devoted personal maid proceeded to London Airport and in a few hours were in the air. Emma, as usual, was sick, but the old lady was as hard as nails, and stepped out at the other end of the trip as fresh as if she had taken a bus ride.

After six weeks of almost unbroken sunshine Lady Wimster was quite ready to go back to her delectable house, and was planning a party or two to celebrate her return. They made the swift journey home, and at the railway station which was three miles from her house Lady Wimster saw Sergeant Kent just as she and Emma were getting into a taxi. The Sergeant touched his helmet and then came along to the taxi.

'Glad to see you back again, my lady,' he said. 'Hope you had a pleasant holiday.'

'Most enjoyable. How's the garden looking?'

'Beautiful. Them herbacious borders are better than I've ever seen 'em, and the lawn's like a carpet. Nice lot of fruit coming on too.'

'Good! I've missed the sight of a really nice lawn. They don't do these things so well abroad. Thank you for everything.'

'A pleasure, my lady.'

The taxi moved away and in a short time it was rolling up the drive towards the house. Lady Wimster looked out at the garden and nodded her head.

'Evans has done well,' she said. 'He's a dear man. I'm glad I remembered to bring him a present.'

It was one of Evans's gardening days, and he emerged from a shrubbery as the taxi came to a standstill, touched his hat and came forward to lend a hand with the baggage.

'The garden's lovely, Evans,' said Lady Wimster. 'I've never seen it look so well.'

Old Evans smiled and took the key from Lady Wimster, while she paid the driver. Emma and Evans then entered the house and carried the various suitcases into their appropriate bedrooms. Lady Wimster went into the lounge, and then uttered a piercing shriek. Evans ran downstairs, and found her leaning against the door post gesticulating speechlessly. Evans's gaze went to the beautifully furnished room and then he saw the cause of her ladyship's alarm, for lying on the floor, face downwards, was a man. He made to go forward, but was assailed by a dreadful odour. Quickly he closed the door.

'I – I must telephone the police,' he said. 'Miss Paston, you'd better take her ladyship to her room.'

'No,' said Lady Wimster. 'I'm all right. But call the police. Emma, I think we need a cup of tea.'

It was a very shame-faced Sergeant Kent, who finally saw Lady Wimster in the morning room. He had seen the corpse and was as horrified as she was.

'I've telephoned to headquarters,' he said. 'The ambulance and some officers are on their way now. The body has been there for a long time – weeks. I assure your ladyship I visited the house every day personally· I found nothing to indicate a break-in. Has anything been stolen?'

'Emma says she can find nothing missing, and no sign of any disturbance in any of the other rooms.'

'I'm terribly sorry, my lady.'

'I'm not blaming you, Sergeant. It could have happened to anybody, but it's a great mystery all the same. Is there any disturbance in the lounge?'

'None that I could see. But you won't be able to use that room for some time. It will have to be fumigated.'

'Did you discover how the man died?'

'Yes. He was shot twice – in the stomach.'

Lady Wimster winced, and then Emma entered to say

that she had discovered how the man got in. There was a broken pane of glass in a back bedroom which was situated over the low roof of the domestic quarters. The Sergeant went with her to look at this, and then Lady Wimster went to her bedroom.

The ambulance and the investigation officers arrived soon after. The sergeant made his report, and Emma and the gardener were questioned, while the police surgeon performed his thankless task. Finally the body – wrapped up with the tightness of a mummy – was removed, and the room thoroughly disinfected, and sealed. The investigating officer saw Lady Wimster before he left.

'So far we haven't been able to establish the man's identity,' he said. 'We haven't even tried because the body is in a terrible state. Medical evidence is that it has been here three weeks at least.'

'Shocking!'

'Yes. I will communicate with you if and when we establish his identity. In the meantime if you should discover that anything is missing from the house please inform me.'

Lady Wimster promised to do this, but search as she might she could not discover that a single thing had been removed, nor any drawers or cupboards interfered with. That evening she heard from Sergeant Kent that the celebrated Inspector McLean was coming from London the next morning to take over the case.

'Oh dear!' she sighed. 'The house will be full of detectives for weeks to come. Why did it have to happen to me. Emma, has that new lot of notepaper arrived? I want to write some letters.'

'It's coming tomorrow,' said Emma. 'The printers rang up and said they tried to deliver it two days ago, but found the house locked up.'

It was on the following morning that Lady Wimster, just finishing her breakfast, was told by Emma that the housekeeper was back and that Inspector McLean, of Scotland Yard, and another officer were in the hall, waiting to see her.

'Take them into the study,' she said. 'I won't keep them a few minutes.'

Lady Wimster eventually found McLean and Sergeant Brook gazing through the wide study windows at the colourful garden, and obviously appreciating it. 'I'm sorry to keep you waiting, officers,' she said. 'This is a shocking business. Please be seated.'
'I have seen the evidence already taken,' said McLean, and I have just come from the mortuary. While searching for anything which might help to establish the dead man's identity, this letter was found in his coat pocket. It's in a bad state, so I won't ask you to handle it.'
He produced a folded and blood-stained letter, which bore Lady Wimster's embossed address at the top. It was not dated, and the context was typewritten. McLean read it:

'*Dear Ronald,*
Your letter to the old address has been forwarded here, where I am now living, hence the delay in answering it. I shall be delighted to see you on Friday next, at eight-thirty in the evening. Don't trouble to reply if that is okay. I've no doubt we can come to terms.
Yours,
Chaffy.'

He held the letter up so that Lady Wimster could see it. She produced a lorgnette and peered through it.
'Chaffy,' she said. 'There is no one here named Chaffy.'
'It sounds rather like a nickname. Is there anyone who might be called that?'
'No. There is only Emma my maid, and the housekeeper. There's another thing too. When I went away I took the small supply of notepaper which I had left. I had previously ordered a new supply, and that hasn't yet been delivered. So that letter must have been written before I went away – six weeks ago.'
'That doesn't accord with the facts,' said McLean. 'It must have been written a few days before the man was murdered. That is to say less than a month ago.'
'You mean it was written in this house?'
'It could have been. Is there a typewriter here?'
'Yes. I use it when I have business letters to write. I didn't take it with me.'

'I should like to see it.'

Lady Wimster produced the small typewriter from under a table. McLean took off the cover, and then removed the spools and ribbon. The latter was a new one, and he could see the last impressions made. The word 'Chaffy' was quite clear.

'Yes, it was typed with this machine,' he said. 'The question is how someone got a clean sheet of your note-paper if, as you have stated, there was none in the house.'

'I am certain I took the last sheets away with me. But I don't quite understand. Was that letter written to lure the man who was murdered to this house?'

'Undoubtedly, and the culprit must be someone who knew you were away from home, and possibly knew you had a typewriter. In any case it was necessary for him to disguise his handwriting, and what better than a type-writer. The story about his letter from the dead man hav-ing been forwarded here makes clear his intentions. It was cool and calculated murder, which he knew was unlikely to be discovered for several weeks.'

After a few more questions about the integrity of the servants, whom Lady Wimster vouched for, McLean opened up the lounge, and he and Brook spent some time there. The place reeked with disinfectant and where the dead man had lain there was a horrid dark stain. But otherwise the room was in perfect order. The ash-trays were all clean, and the various cushions were all neatly arranged. McLean knew that the County Police had looked for any ejected cartridge cases, without success, but he and Brook had another search, and finally reached the conclusion that they must have been retrieved by the murderer, since it was now established that the weapon used was an automatic.

'Nothing here,' he said. 'We'll try to trace his progress through that broken window.'

Here they were a little more successful, for there was a footprint on the flower bed under the window through which entry had been made and some disturbance of the moss on the tiles over which the intruder had crawled, but neither of these traces could be called 'clues', for the footprint was imperfect and the moss could have been disturbed by birds.

'He had to come twice, hadn't he?' asked Brook. 'Once

to use the typewriter, and then later to keep the appointment.'

'Yes, but on the first visit he could have unbolted the back door, and taken the key away with him, to make his second entry easy. We know almost nothing about him, except that his Christian name was undoubtedly Ronald. Our best line of approach is through that sheet of notepaper. Where did he get hold of that?'

'There's the printer,' suggested Brook.

'Yes. I hadn't overlooked him.'

Later they went into the nearby town and saw the printer of the letter headings. He was aghast at the bare suggestion that any member of the firm should have used a customer's notepaper for some nefarious purpose, and took McLean to the man who had actually done the embossing. McLean finally came away with the impression that although there was the possibility of leakage there, the odds were greatly against it.

'It is in their favour that according to the manager nobody there knew that Lady Wimster was going away,' said McLean. 'We have to look elsewhere. I should like to question Lady Wimster's personal maid.'

'But she was with her mistress all the time.'

'Yes, but she may come into this business –innocently.'

When they got back to the house McLean saw Emma alone.

'Have you at any time used Lady Wimster's notepaper?' he asked.

'Not for my personal correspondence.'

'But you have on matters concerning the household?'

'Yes, once or twice.'

'To whom?'

'It's difficult to remember. I certainly wrote to Harrods some time ago, giving them a list of books, which she had copied from a Sunday newspaper, and which she wanted put on her library list. On another occasion I wrote to a firm who were advertising a list of garden plants, but I can't remember the name.'

'Have you on any occasion written in pencil?'

'No, I don't think so. I have a ball-pointed pen of my own.'

'You have been with Lady Wimster a long time, I believe?'

'Over twenty years. I came to her when I was quite a young girl.'

'Do you use the typewriter here?'

'No. I've never learned to type.'

McLean was not certain that he had drawn a blank, for there was something a little furtive in Emma's demeanour, and just the slightest hesitation in her replies. When she had gone he drew out the letter, examined the folded edges and held it up to the light.

'I can't help thinking that this letter heading was used twice,' he said. 'There's a disturbed look about the surface. If a hard pencil were used and the writing erased it might have that effect. We'll see what the laboratory can make of it.'

The next day the experts with their special powders, and camera lenses made quite a lot of it. The sheet of paper had been written on prior to having been used in a typewriter, and from some of the broken impression they made words. One sentence came out very clearly. It said:

'—thank you for the lovely Cupid box. It is—'

McLean was immensely pleased with this. He did not think the very broken writing could be traced definitely to any person, but it would be interesting if someone in Lady Wimster's house had recently acquired a 'Cupid Box', whatever that might be.

An hour later McLean called at the house. He was let in by the housekeeper who informed him that Lady Wimster was not yet up. He asked to see Emma.

'She's gone into the town, sir, to do some early shopping,' said the housekeeper.

'I want to look into the bedrooms,' said McLean. 'Please ask her ladyship if that is convenient. I don't wish to see her room.'

Lady Wimster was quite agreeable, and McLean and Brook went up the broad staircase with the housekeeper, who indicated the various rooms.

'Lady Wimster's is the first on the right,' she said. 'Mine is next, and Emma's is the last. The bedrooms on the other side are spare ones.'

McLean nodded, passed her ladyship's room, and

entered the housekeeper's. The bed had already been made, and the room was quite tidy. McLean looked for any sort of box which might fit the description but found none. He then came out and passed into Emma's room, which was in contrast to the housekeeper's sober sanctuary. There were nick-nacks everywhere, and right in the centre of the dressing-table was a small siver box inlaid with porcelain, depicting Cupid with his conventional bow and arrow.

'There it is,' said McLean.

'So Emma wrote that letter – and lied about it?'

'She may have really forgotten that she wrote it in pencil, but she lied about not using Lady Wimster's note-paper for her own correspondence.'

McLean opened the box. It contained pins of various types, and a couple of brooches.

'Are you going to question her?' asked Brook.

'Not if I can find her friend's address. We do not know how she will react. She might warn him.'

He commenced opening drawers, and finally he found a bundle of letters. They were all couched in affectionate terms, and bore an address in Woking, the nearby town. All were signed 'Mortimer' and the most recent of them referred to her pending trip to Madeira, and his sorrow at the prospect of separation for so long a time. McLean compared the writing with the single written word on the typewritten letter. It was identical.

'We'll leave out Emma for the moment,' he said. 'Let's get across to Woking.'

III

At the Woking address McLean met with a disappointment. When he located the house he saw a notice board to the effect that the house having been sold privately, the furniture would be offered for auction the following week. He thereupon told Brook to drive to the house agent whose address was given. It was only a few minutes away.

Here he was informed that the late occupant had rented the place furnished, and had left suddenly about three weeks previously. The owner had decided not to let the property again.

'What was the last occupier's name?' asked McLean.

'Mortimer Finch. He was a widower, back from the East. He lived at the house for about a year.'

'Have you any idea where he can be found?'

'None at all. I wish I had, because the owner was entitled to a month's notice, or rent in lieu of same.'

'Is the owner available?'

'No. He is in America. I cabled him and he instructed us to sell the place.'

It was only when they were back in the car that Brook had a brainwave.

'Finch,' he said. 'Why, that's the meaning of "Chaffy". He was known to certain people by that nickname. Short for Chaffinch.'

McLean smiled and Brook knew that he was a little late in the uptake.

'Well, where do we go from here?' he asked.

'Back to Lady Wimster's. I am going to have a heart to heart talk with her maid – Emma.'

Emma was in when McLean reached the house, and McLean saw her in the study. She looked far from happy, but McLean thought that was due to the white lie she had told about the notepaper.

'Do you know a man named Mortimer Finch?' asked McLean.

'Y-yes.'

'Did he give you a silver box some time ago?'

'Yes – on my birthday.'

'Are you in love with this man?'

Emma hesitated, and finally nodded.

'When did you last see him?'

'Just before I went away with her ladyship.'

'Do you know where he is now?'

'No.'

McLean thought she was lying, and then produced the typewritten letter.

'This sheet of notepaper was used by you to thank Finch for the gift of the Cupid box. You must have written in pencil, which Finch erased. He used this same sheet of notepaper to lure to this house the man who was shot here. I must warn you that if you are shielding this man you may be charged as an accessory after the fact.'

66

Emma's face was as pale as a sheet, and her eyes expressed the horror she undoubtedly felt.

'Now,' said McLean. 'Do you know where Finch can be found?'

Emma hesitated and then burst into tears. McLean waited patiently until the storm had abated.

'I – I told the truth just now,' she said. 'I don't know where he is. I wrote to his old address but the letter was returned. Then yesterday – he rang me up. He – he asked me to meet him tonight.'

'Where?' asked McLean.

'At the main bookstall on Waterloo Station – at six o'clock. Lady Wimster has give me the evening off.'

'I want you to help us – to identify this man.'

Emma begged to be excused. She wanted to do the right thing, but this was too much. She had a photograph in her handbag. Wouldn't that do?

McLean, on seeing the very clear photograph, was agreeable. At a few minutes before six o'clock he and Brook were at the bookstall, pretending to be interested in the display. Then came the handsome but rather sinister man of the photograph. McLean approached him.

'Are you Mr. Mortimer Finch?' he asked.

'No. My name is Watson.'

McLean gave Brook a glance, and they sandwiched the man between them.

'We are police officers,' said McLean. 'Come quietly with us to that car, or we shall have to handcuff you.'

Finch went quietly enough. At Scotland Yard he was searched, and among other things a loaded automatic was taken from him. Later the bullets extracted from the dead man were traced to the weapon. Finch seemed to realize it was all up, but he refused to make any statement and was then formally charged with murder. McLean now concentrated in establishing the identity of the murdered man, and a week later he came to Brook with some papers and photographs in his hands.

'There they are,' he said. 'Finch and a man named Ronald Jeens. Convicts in the same prison at Nantes. Finch escaped about a year ago, but Jeens served out his sentence, and came to England last December.'

'Blackmail?'

'Yes. He could have put Finch back in prison, and Finch didn't like that prospect. Well, that's a nice job done!'

7

AT the little ferry port of Lymington the evening boat from the Isle of Wight arrived in a half gale accompanied by driving sleet. There were five cars and their occupants, and about a dozen other passengers. The squat little boat was tied up and the passengers filed off into the darkness. The cars left last, and finally only one remained – a small Standard saloon. The disembarkation officer went up to the car, expecting to see the driver at the wheel, but to his surprise the car was empty, except for several suitcases piled on the back seat.

'Find that driver, Harry,' he called to a seaman. 'He must be up in the refreshment room. I want to get ashore.'

But the owner of the car could not be found, and soon it was obvious that he was not on the ferry-boat, for only the normal crew and the woman who ran the refreshment bar remained.

'This is a fine how d'yer do.' said the officer. 'A man wouldn't go off and leave his car behind.'

'How do you know it was a man?' asked Harry. 'It might have been a woman.'

'It was a man. I remember him when he drove the car aboard. Dark fellow of about forty years of age, wearing a mackintosh and a beret. We'll have to get on to the police. Looks mighty like suicide to me.'

The police were duly informed. They took the car into custody and very soon established that the owner was a Mr. James Duffy, of an address in Battersea. The case was handed to Inspector McLean at Scotland Yard, but before he could do anything a telephone message came from the Hampshire police to inform him that a body had been recovered from the sea, and that letters in a pocket gave the name of James Duffy. The medical evidence was that he had been struck a violent blow on the head before he entered the water.

'So it wasn't suicide,' mused McLean. 'Brook, we shall have to go down to Lymington where the body is lying. But first of all we'll try to find someone who can identify him. Drive me to the Battersea address.'

A little later McLean rang the bell at a first-floor flat not far from the river. There was no reply after many rings, so McLean went to the lower flat and rang the bell there. An elderly woman answered the door.

'I am a police officer,' said McLean. 'Do you know the man who occupies the upstairs flat?'

'Mr. Duffy? Oh yes, but he's away for a few days.'

'Does he live alone?'

'Yes. I think he lost his wife two years ago – just before he took the flat.'

'Is he engaged in business?'

'Yes. I think he is a traveller for some big firm, but I don't know the name of the firm. Sometimes he's away for days on end. When he is he leaves his door-key with me, so that I can feed his cat. She can get in and out through a window which he leaves open, and I leave some milk for her every day.'

'Have you the key now?'

'Yes.'

McLean explained the position and then asked for the loan of the key as he was anxious to trace any relatives of the dead man. She brought the key and McLean and Sergeant Brook opened the upstairs flat. It was a small place, but excellently furnished and very clean and tidy. A search provided the information which McLean needed immediately. He found some business cards showing that Duffy was employed by a big firm of manufacturing jewellers in Clerkenwell, and also a letter dated a week previously from a woman who signed herself 'Fanny' and whom he believed to be Duffy's sister. Her address was in Kensington.

Half an hour later he and Brook were closeted with Mrs. Fanny Wood – the sister of the dead man, who received the news of her brother's death with horror and tears. McLean waited for her to recover.

'Did you know that your brother had gone to the Isle of Wight?' he asked.

'No. I never know where he is as he travels about so much.'

'When did you last see him?'

'Three weeks ago. He and I and my husband went to a show together.'

'Was he a widower?'

'Yes – for the past two years.'

'Do you know of any reason why anyone should assault him, or seek his life?'

'No – none at all.'

'When you last saw him did he appear to be quite happy?'

'Yes, quite his usual self. He was always very high-spirited. He told me he was doing very well in his job, and on that evening we were his guests.'

'No current love affairs?'

'I don't think so. He was very much in love with his wife, and when she died it was a terrible blow to him. But after a year or so he got over it.'

McLean asked her if she would be willing to identify the dead man and she consented. She was taken at once by road to Lymington and there identified her brother at once. McLean, who had work to do on the spot put her on a train and thanked her. A little later he had a talk with the doctor who had made the post-mortem.

'The blow on the head was not mortal,' he said. 'It may have rendered him temporarily unconscious, but certainly would not have killed him. He actually died from drowning.'

'What sort of an implement was it?'

'Not metal, in my opinion. Possibly a heavy walking-stick, with a bulbous handle. He was struck from behind, and the blow was softened by the fact that he was wearing a black beret, according to witnesses who saw him before he vanished. But I expect you know that.'

McLean nodded. He had no more questions to ask, and proceeded to County Police Headquarters where he saw the car. The suitcases which it contained had been opened. There was nothing in them but clothing. This surprised McLean, who had imagined that at least one of the cases would contain samples of jewellery.

'It looks as if his trip to the island was not a business one,' he said. 'Perhaps his clothing may help to explain his reasons for going there.'

But the clothing when produced revealed nothing in

the nature of hotel receipts. There was a wallet containing fifteen pounds in money, some business cards, a bunch of keys, and two counterfoils of a theatre in Ventnor.

'We'll try the Ventnor hotels,' said McLean. 'He may have stayed there and torn up the receipt.'

But no hotel in Ventnor knew anything about Mr. Duffy, and during the day all the principal hotels in the island were tried with no success at all.

II

The case now looked extremely difficult. McLean got through to the firm who employed Duffy, and was told that he had left his samples with them on the previous Friday, and was taking a week's holiday. They had no idea where he proposed to spend it.

'What do we do now?' asked Brook. 'Not a blessed clue of any sort. And how did he get murdered on a small boat like that without anyone knowing it?'

'It was dark,' said McLean. 'And the evidence is that nearly all the passengers were in the refreshment room sheltering from the wind and rain. Mr. Duffy apparently wasn't, nor was the man who murdered him. Our job is made extremely difficult by the absence of witnesses. I'm going to try to get them all together.'

'You mean all the passengers who were on the boat?'

'Yes.'

That night a police message went out over the B.B.C. It requested all the passengers who had been on the ferry at that particular crossing to communicate with Scotland Yard as soon as possible. The broadcast was repeated again the next day, and one by one the replies came in. McLean was gratified with the quick response.

'I've got them all but one,' he said. 'Most of them are in the south, but a few are farther north. I must be satisfied with that. The thing now is to get them here in a bunch.'

'Asking rather a lot, isn't it?'

'Yes, but when they know what is at stake I think they will co-operate.'

All this took time to arrange, and while it was being completed McLean saw the manager of the firm who had employed Duffy. He was unable to advance any theory

71

whatsoever. The firm had some customers on the island, but since Duffy had visited them only a month previously there was no need for him to go again so soon afterwards. He knew very little of Duffy's private life, beyond the fact that his wife had died two years previously.

'A very good salesman,' he said. 'He had the whole of the south-east area. He had been with us for fifteen years. I wish I could help, Inspector, but we here are all completely mystified.'

Then at last came the meeting with the passengers, and the other persons who had been on the ferry with Duffy. McLean had secured recent photographs of the dead man, and a number of the witnesses recognized him – the woman in the refreshment room in particular.

'I remember serving him with a Guinness,' she said. 'The room was full. I think almost everyone was present at first, but later Duffy left.'

'That's right,' said an elderly man. 'I had gone to the refreshment room for a coffee, but only stayed a few minutes. It was very smoky and I went and sat in my car. I saw him come down the steps and walk along the deck towards the stern. I noticed the beret he was wearing, and thought it very sensible in the conditions.'

'Did you see anyone else on deck at the time?'

'Not at the time, but a little earlier there was a man pacing the deck, as if he enjoyed the wind and rain. He appeared to be crippled, for he walked with the aid of a stick.'

'Are you sure of that?' asked McLean.

'Yes. I saw him later when he got off the boat. He was carrying just a small suitcase.'

Two other passengers now recalled the limping man with the walking-stick, and all eyes went round the seated throng.

'Would you know him again?' McLean asked.

The elderly man said he thought he would.

'Is he present?' asked McLean.

The witness gazed at all the tense faces.

'No,' he said. 'I'm certain he's not here.'

'I think I can tell you now that one of the passengers did not respond to our broadcast appeals. He may well be the man you mention. Can you tell me anything about him?'

'I think he was above average height. He wore a dark rain-coat – not a mackintosh, and a dark felt hat. As he came under a light I saw that he had a tiny dark moustache. Perhaps forty years of age.'

Finally the meeting broke up, and McLean warmly thanked those who had come at considerable inconvenience. When they were all gone he revealed his satisfaction.

'Not a very intelligent man, our murderer,' he said. 'He made two mistakes. The first was that he should have gone off in Duffy's car, which would have made our case almost impossibly difficult. The second is that he should have responded to our appeal and come here boldly to give evidence.'

'He might not have heard the broadcast,' argued Brook.

'That's possible, but not probable. Anyway it is significant that he carried the sort of implement which knocked out Duffy, and apparently did not put in an appearance in the refreshment room, perhaps for fear of coming face to face with Duffy. Now we have to find him.'

Brook looked down his nose, for it seemed to him they had no jumping off place. But McLean was far from being pessimistic, and within half an hour he and Brook were on their way to Ventnor.

'Trying the hotels again, sir?' he asked.

'No. I am interested in those two theatre counterfoils. Duffy went to a theatre with a friend. That friend is our best bet if we can find him.'

They crossed to Ryde, taking the car with them, and from there drove to Ventnor. It was the end of the holiday season and visitors were few. The theatre was still open and McLean went to the box office where an intelligent looking woman was in charge.

'I am a police officer,' he said. 'And I am trying to trace two persons who used these tickets last Thursday evening. Can you help me?'

The woman took the counterfoils, and then went to a file and produced a chart for the day in question. McLean saw that only about half the seats in the stalls were scored across in red pencil.

'Row E. Numbers nine and ten,' mused the woman.

'These two seats were reserved by telephone and picked up the following day.'

'Any name?' asked McLean.

'Yes. The name written here is Shelton, of Acton.'

'Where is Acton?'

'It's about three miles westward, on the coast. Just a small hamlet.'

'Do you recall the people who took up the tickets?'

'I'm sorry, but at the time I was very busy. I think it was a man and a woman.'

McLean had to be satisfied with that. He and Brook went off in the car to Acton. It was a pleasant little hamlet, situated on a southern slope, with a public house, a general store, and a number of cottages and farms. McLean stopped the car outside the pub.

'We'll have a drink,' he said.

The publican welcomed them and served them with two tankards of ale.

'Is there anyone named Shelton living here?' asked McLean.

'Yes sir, at the pink cottage near the sea. Mr. Shelton bought the cottage three years ago, but he and his wife only come here for holidays.'

'Are they here now?'

'I don't think so. Mrs. Shelton was here last week, but I think she left a few days ago.'

'Was she with her husband?'

'She may have been, but I didn't see him.'

'Is he a crippled gentleman?'

'No, sir. Far from it. He's very athletic and a fine swimmer.'

McLean said no more, but a few minutes later he and Brook were ringing the bell at the immaculate pink cottage. There was no response, and McLean was soon convinced that the place was vacant. He went to the garage and peered through the small window. There was no car inside. Round by the back door there was a dustbin. McLean opened the lid. It was half full of refuse, and with some soiled newspapers was a sheet of brown paper. On this was written, Mrs. E. Shelton, The Firs, Radstock, Nr. Chichester. This had been crossed out, and the present address written in large capitals.

'Our next port of call is Radstock,' said McLean.

74

It was late in the afternoon when they reached 'The Firs.' It was a well-built luxury house lying back in a fine garden, and a smart domestic answered the bell. McLean asked to see Mrs. Shelton and was ultimately shown into a room where an attractive woman of about thirty-five was waiting.

'I am a police officer,' said McLean. 'I believe that you stayed at your cottage in the Isle of Wight last week?'

'Yes. I have only been back three days. Don't tell me I have been burgled?'

'Oh no. Did you stay there alone?'

'Yes. My husband had to go to Exeter on business for ten days, and that left me high and dry. So I decided to go to the cottage.'

'Last Thursday you went to the theatre at Ventnor?'

'Yes.'

'Alone?'

'What a strange question to ask!'

'It is a very necessary question. Who was your companion?'

'A man I know. But I don't see—'

'Was his name Duffy? This man?'

McLean suddenly produced the photograph of Duffy, and Mrs. Shelton went pallid.

'Yes,' she stammered.

'Mrs. Shelton,' said McLean. 'Duffy was murdered on the car ferry on his way back to the mainland.'

The effect of this upon Mrs. Shelton was tremendous. She closed her eyes and groped wildly. Brook went to her aid and helped her to a chair.

'When did you last see Duffy?' asked McLean.

'On Friday evening. He – he drove in his car to catch the ferry.'

'Had he been staying with you?'

'Y-yes.'

'Did your husband know of this affair?'

'No. He was away from home a great deal, and I was lonely.'

'Where is your husband now?'

'Still in Exeter. I had a letter from him this morning. He is coming home today. Here is the letter.'

She produced a letter from her handbag. It was brief but quite affectionate. It was written on hotel notepaper, and stated that he hoped to leave Exeter after lunch and to be home for dinner.

'I'll wait for him – in my car,' said McLean.

It was half an hour later when a luxurious and powerful car entered the drive and stopped at the front door. A man stepped out of it, and stared at the police car. McLean got out and went to him.

'Are you Mr. Shelton?' he asked.

'Yes. Did you want me?'

'I am a police officer, and am making inquiries about a man named James Duffy who met his death recently. Do you know the man?'

'No.'

'I understand you have been staying in Exeter, at the Newton Hotel. How long were you there?'

'Ten days in all. I am converting a house there, and there was some little trouble.'

'You stayed at the hotel all the time?'

'Yes, between the hotel and the building site which is some two miles away.'

'Did you know your wife had spent some time at your seaside cottage?'

'No. But she sometimes did that.'

'And you are sure you do not know Mr. Duffy?'

'Quite sure. I have never met anyone of that name.'

'Then I'm sorry to have troubled you,' said McLean.

McLean drove back to Scotland Yard in a reflective mood. Was Shelton the murderer? The circumstances and the motive favoured that conclusion, but not the physical description. There was no trace of lameness – no moustache. But both these things could have been deliberately faked. He decided to take up the alibi at once, and made a speedy trip to Exeter.

Here it was established that Shelton had slept in the hotel every night since his arrival there, and his story about a house conversion was true. But it was a little significant that on the day of the murder Shelton had not been seen at the hotel between noon and midnight.

'A man with a fast car could have got to the island and back in that interval,' mused McLean. 'But he would have to go by the Lymington crossing, and take a taxi on the other side.'

'But he had his car,' said Brook.

'That's the point. It's quite a good point too. We'll go back by Lymington.'

At Lymington McLean called at the main garage and saw the proprietor.

'I suppose that some people going over to the island by the ferry leave their cars here?' he asked.

'Oh yes. It's quite expensive taking a car across.'

'Do you keep records?'

'Yes.'

'Then can you tell me if you garaged a Bentley car here – registration MUO 309 – last Friday afternoon or evening?'

'I can tell you without looking,' said the man. 'The car was left here at about five o'clock. It was painted green and was collected by the owner after the arrival of the last ferry from Yarmouth.'

'Would you recognize him again?'

'I'm sure I should.'

'Did he take a walking-stick with him?'

'That's curious. He did take a heavy walking-stick with him when he left the car, but when he came back he didn't appear to have the stick.'

'Thank you!' said McLean. 'I may ask you to identify a man later.'

This identification took place at Scotland Yard the following day, when the garage proprietor faced a line of twelve men, and without hesitation picked out Shelton.

'So he threw the walking-stick overboard,' said Brook, later.

'I think so, and his spurious little moustache. He was clever up to a point, but not quite clever enough.'

8

Sergeant Brook was enormously proud of his new television set.

'Miles better than the old one,' he said. 'Nice big

picture, and none of that fading at the corners. You must come and see it one evening.'

McLean promised to do so, but for a long time was prevented by one thing and another. Brook, anxious to display his new toy, dropped an unmistakable hint one morning.

'Gorgeous fight on tonight,' he said. 'Can't wait to get home. Good as a ten-guinea ring seat. It's a pity—'

'All right, Brook,' said McLean. 'I know what you're driving at. I'll come and join you if I may.'

'Fine!' said Brook.

McLean went round to Brook's flat just before the time the fight was due to start. Brook had the set switched on and nicely tuned in. The reception was certainly excellent, and the promoter was busy introducing boxing personalities to the spectators. From time to time the camera roved round, and McLean recognized a great number of public figures.

'Clear as a bell,' said Brook.

'Yes, very good indeed.'

At last the contestants came on and were introduced amid great applause. Then, finally, the fight commenced. It proved to be a tremendous battle, with a great deal of gore. Brook, who loved nothing better than a fight, made a commentary of his own.

'I've got a quid on the Birmingham lad,' he said. 'He'll finish it in the ninth round. You mark my words.'

'I don't think he'll be on his feet in the ninth round,' said McLean. 'He's wide open for an upper cut.'

At the end of the fifth round the Birmingham lad took the uppercut, and that was the end of that. The scene changed and McLean found himself watching an incredibly silly game, fit only for adolescents of substandard intelligence, but he kept his opinion to himself out of courtesy to his host.

It was ten days after this event that the body of a young woman was taken from the river just below Richmond. She was clad in a rather abbreviated swim-suit, and the medical evidence was that she had been in the water about three hours. The curious thing was that no clothing which might have belonged to her had been found, and so for the moment her identity was unknown.

The police took the view that she had bathed from

the grounds of a riverside house, which would account for the absent clothing, and they expected an early report on a missing woman. But a full day passed, and no report came.

'A curious case,' McLean said to Brook. 'She has a ring on her engagement finger, and the medical evidence is that some attempt was made shortly before death to remove it, but the ring was very tight and would not come off.'

'She might have tried to remove it herself,' said Brook.

'She might, but a post mortem is now taking place to make sure that there was no dirty work.'

'You mean a drug or something?'

'There's that possibility. If one wanted to cover up someone's identity it might be a good idea to render her unconscious, destroy her clothing and consign her to the river.'

It was a little later when a woman came to Scotland Yard to report that her daughter had been missing from home for two days. The description she gave was not unlike that of the unfortunate drowned girl, and McLean asked her if she would go with him to see the body.

She agreed to do this but, before taking her, a message came from the doctor who had just carried out the post mortem. It was to the effect that the girl had undoubtedly been heavily drugged before she met her death.

'Just as you said, sir,' said Brook.

'I didn't. It was just an obvious possibility. Now I must take Mrs. Andrews along.'

It was the first time that McLean had seen the body. It had not the unsightly appearance of the average drowned person, because only a small amount of water was in the lungs. The features were well balanced, and the hair luxurious. Mrs. Andrews came forward and stared at the reposeful dead face.

'No – no, sir,' she murmured. 'That's not my daughter – thank God!'

McLean took another long look at the face before it was covered up and then took Mrs. Andrews back to the waiting car. He returned later to Scotland Yard in a reflective mood.

'Was it the woman's daughter, sir?' asked Brook.

'No. It's a curious thing but I've a feeling I've met that girl somewhere, and not very long ago. She's not the ordinary type. Beautiful but just a little on the coarse side. I wish I could place her.'

No one else came forward in reply to the police broadcast. The coroner's inquest took place, and an open verdict was returned. Two days passed and Mrs. Andrews's daughter came back to her, with a story that no one but a fond mother would believe.

'Well, she's off our books,' said McLean. 'I wish I could remember where I saw that other poor girl.'

Then suddenly, while he was having a meal, McLean's normally excellent memory for faces functioned. He had a vision of the girl sitting beside a hook-nosed man, and of bright lights. He swallowed his coffee in a gulp and hurried back to the office.

'I think I've got it, Brook,' he said. 'That dead girl's face. Something clicked and there she was. Remember the fight which we saw on your TV set?'

'I always remember when I've lost a quid.'

'She was at the fight – near the ring, dressed very nicely for the occasion. Two or three times the camera brought her into view, and I couldn't help noticing her, because she was almost the only woman in the nearer seats. I expect there was a telefilm made.'

'There was,' said Brook. 'It was showing last week at my local cinema.'

'Good! We'll take another look at it.'

II

Some hours later McLean and Brook were seated in the private projection room of a film-producing company. The film started to run, but between the second and third rounds of the fight McLean stopped it at the point where it was ranging round the nearer seats. There was the dead girl, talking to the man with the hooked nose. A little later he came away with some enlarged prints of the actual scene.

'Find the man with the beak,' he said, 'and we may make some progress. He looks rather like an old bruiser.'

'One of the boxing critics is almost sure to know him,' said Brook.

So will the promoter. We'll try him first.'

At his flat off Piccadilly Joe Chandler, who had promoted the fight, stared at the photograph.

'I don't know the girl,' he said, 'but the man she's talking to is Ben Logan; pretty good as a cruiser weight a few years back. Now keeps a pub in Hoxton called the Blue Boar.'

Half an hour later McLean and Brook saw Logan in the flesh. The pub had recently been enlarged, and had all the evidence of prosperity. It was not yet opening time for the evening session and Logan was in his private sitting-room, reading the *Sporting Times.* McLean showed him the enlarged photograph.

'Do you recognize that?' he asked.

'Sure I do,' said Logan. 'It's me at the White City fight.'

'Did you go there alone?'

'Yes. I'm not married, and I go to all the fights I can. Used to be in the game myself.'

'Who is the girl next to you?'

'I don't know.'

'But she spoke to you, didn't she?'

'Yes. We got talking between rounds. She asked me who I thought would win, and I told her I had my money on the coloured boy. There was a vacant seat on her right, and she told me that she was expecting a friend to join her, but he hadn't turned up.'

'Anything else?'

'Yes. When the fight was over it began to rain. I went to get my car and found her trying to get a taxi, but there was no hope. I asked her if I could give her a lift, and she told me she lived in Cumberland Terrace. I said I could drop her there as I had to pass quite close to the place.'

'And you took her?'

'Yes. She got out at the third house on the left as you enter the terrace. She thanked me and I drove on.'

'You had never seen her before?'

'Never.'

'Did she give you no clue to the man she was expecting?'

'None at all.'

McLean had no difficulty in finding the house mentioned by Logan. It had once been a fine family house but was now converted into three flats. There was a name plate in the hall. The ground floor and the second floor were in the occupation of a doctor and a dentist respectively, but the top floor's occupant was given as Miss Studeley.

'No lift,' sighed Brook. 'Do we go up, sir?'

'Yes.'

They trudged up two rather steep flights of stairs and ultimately reached a door which bore the visiting card of Miss Ida Studeley. McLean rang the bell several times, but got no response. He then went down to the lower flat and rang the bell there. The door was opened by a young woman who was obviously the doctor's receptionist. As the doctor was engaged with a patient McLean put his questions to the receptionist.

'Yes, I know Miss Studeley slightly,' she said.

McLean then showed her the photograph.

'Is this the lady?' he asked.

'Yes.'

'Have you seen her recently?'

'Yes. Two days ago. I met her on the stairs – lower down. I was coming up and she was going out.'

'Who is the actual owner of the flat?'

'Doctor Osborne – my employer.'

In view of this McLean decided to wait to see Osborne. When the doctor was free he said he had bought the house three years previously, and had sublet the top and the bottom floors. He had spare keys of both apartments. McLean explained the situation to him, and the doctor handed him the spare key.

McLean opened up the top flat. It was very small, but had a quite commodious sitting-room. The wardrobe in the bedroom was full of expensive dresses and coats, but nowhere could he find any indication of what Miss Studeley had done for a living, if she had had any occupation. The complete absence of letters and documents was a little puzzling, but in the kitchen McLean found what he believed was an explanation. In the small stove a lot of paper had been burnt, and on the top of the ashes was the corner of an envelope which had not been completely consumed. The stamp was franked at a time when the girl was known to be dead.

82

'So someone came here and burnt anything which was likely to help us,' he mused. 'He had a key to the door, probably taken from the girl's handbag. Very clever!'

'It certainly makes things difficult,' grumbled Brook.

McLean's last find was not by any means dramatic, but it aroused his deepest interest. There was a book lying on the bedside table, with a piece of thin cardboard projecting from the pages to mark the place. He opened the book and took up the card.

'A guarantee for a "Sunray" gold and platinum wristwatch,' he said. 'Dated last May. There's a number here, which is probably the serial number of the watch. Purchased from Tysons of Bond Street.'

'I know those watches,' said Brook. 'They cost a pile of money.'

'The question is – where's the watch?'

'You think she was wearing it when she was murdered?'

'Either that, or the murderer took it away when he came here and destroyed letters. There's just one other possibility. She may have taken it back to the shop for some adjustment.'

'Or sold it.'

'Don't spoil my hope. We'll try the jewellers first.'

III

At Tysons McLean was informed that the watch had not come in for repair under the guarantee. At McLean's request the firm's sales records were turned up for the date in question.

'Here we are,' said the manager. 'May the fifteenth. The watch number is quoted. Sold for cash – eighty guineas.'

'Not a cheque?'

'No. Spot cash.'

'Can I see the assistant who made the sale?'

After a little delay a young woman was brought into the office. The manager showed her the counterfoil and asked if she could remember the transaction.

'Yes,' she said. 'It's the only watch of that kind that I've sold. He was a dark, tall gentleman.'

'You are quite sure there wasn't a lady with him?' asked McLean.

'Quite sure. But he's been here again since then. About

a fortnight ago. He had a lady with him then, and bought her an engagement ring.'

'Would you know her again?'

'Oh yes. It was only two days later when I saw her photograph in a society journal. She was Miss Edith Levison. She was mounted on a horse, and it said her father was Master of the Hounds of some hunt.'

McLean then showed her the photograph of the dead woman.

'It this the woman?' he asked.

'Oh no. Not a bit like that. She was very fair with a round face, not a long one.'

McLean waited no longer. Back at his office he turned up a reference book.

'Here he is, I think,' he said to Brook. 'Sir Archibald Levison, chairman of several important companies, and M.F.H. Married 1928. One daughter, named Edith. Shapley Manor, near Woking, Surrey. We'll pay him a visit.'

Sir Archibald looked very puzzled when he received McLean and Brook some time later, in the lounge of his magnificent house.

'What is the trouble, Inspector?' he asked.

'You have a daughter named Edith?'

'Yes. Has she been getting into trouble with her car?'

'No. Did she recently become engaged?'

'No.'

'Could I see her? There is no objection to your being present. I merely want some information from her about a man with whom she is associated.'

Sir Archibald nodded, and pushed a bell. A servant came and was told to tell Miss Edith that her father wished to see her. The girl entered the room a few minutes later. She was pretty and very young.

'Edith,' said her father, 'this gentleman is Inspector McLean. He wishes to ask you some questions.'

The girl smiled and looked at McLean.

'Did you not recently go to a jewellers in Bond Street with a man who bought you an engagement ring?' he asked.

The girl's face became crimson, and she was silent.

'Answer, my dear,' said her father.

'Y—yes,' she stammered·

84

Sir Archibald opened his eyes in astonishment.

'You mean you became engaged to a man without informing me of the fact?' he rasped.

'Yes, father. He asked me to keep it a secret for the time being.'

'Who is the man?'

'Donald Young. I met him months ago at a party. But he's out of a job, and he didn't want to see you until he had fixed himself up in a good post.'

Sir Archibald looked pained and turned to McLean.

'Have you something against this man, Inspector?' he asked.

'I think so, but I can say no more than that at the moment. Miss Levison, where can I find Donald Young?'

'He – he lives in a houseboat, just below Richmond Bridge. It is called *Penelope*.'

It was some hours later that McLean and Brook found the houseboat. The windows were lighted, and the curtains partly drawn. A gangway led from the river bank, and McLean and Brook crossed it and knocked on the door. It was opened by a man of about thirty years of age, with strongly marked features, and bronzed skin.

'Mr. Donald Young?' asked McLean.

'Yes. What do you want?'

'I am a police officer, and should like to ask you a few questions concerning a woman named Studeley.'

'But I know no woman of that name.'

'I think you did. Make way, please.'

They passed into a big saloon where a radiogram was playing softly. McLean switched it off.

'Mr. Young, did you not go to a jewellers in Bond Street last May and buy a "Sunray" watch?'

'No. But I went there recently and bought an engagement ring for my fiancée. There must be some confusion.'

'There is no confusion. You went there twice. For whom did you buy the watch?'

'I bought no watch.'

'I have a witness who will swear that you did. That watch was in Miss Studeley's possession until quite recently, when her dead body was found in the river not far from here. There was an engagement ring on her finger which someone had tried in vain to remove. I suggest you were engaged to Miss Studeley, but grew tired of her when you found another girl, the daughter of a very wealthy man, who was a much better catch. You feared to break off that first engagement because Miss Studeley might say things to Miss Levison which would ruin your chances there. So you lured Miss Studeley here and—'

'It's all a pack of lies,' stormed Young. 'I know nothing of Miss Studeley.'

Brook silenced him by pushing him back into a chair, and then McLean began his search. He did not find the dead woman's clothing nor the watch, but he found something which was as damning. It was a pawn ticket for £25, and later when the ticket was presented McLean found himself in possession of the watch.

'This is the end of Mr. Donald Young,' he said to Brook. 'And to think that if I had not accepted your invitation to see your TV Donald Young might quite likely have got away with it!'

9

IT was George Warren, a farm worker, who found the body of Mrs. Trapping, in the lane leading from her cottage to the farm where he worked. He believed her to be dead, but when the police and a doctor arrived Mrs. Trapping was still breathing although unconscious. She was swiftly removed to the local hospital where she was given a blood transfusion, and now, three hours later Inspector McLean, sent down from London to take over the case, was waiting to know if the transfusion had been successful. The House Surgeon came into the waiting-room.

'Not much hope, I'm afraid,' he said. 'But we should know very quickly now. Horrible business! She was struck at least three heavy blows on the head. It's almost miraculous that she survived them for so long. Not robbery, was it?'

'Apparently not,' said McLean. 'Her handbag was found near the spot. It had six pounds in it.'

'One of our nurses knows her quite well. A very

86

respectable type of woman, liked by everybody. Her husband died three years ago, and left her very little. So she found herself a job in the town. Seems a senseless sort of business, since she's a woman of fifty, and much faded—'

He was interrupted by a nurse, who whispered something to him with a grave face.

'I'll come,' he said. 'Oh, Inspector, I think this is the end, but she may have a few moments of consciousness. I don't know.'

McLean followed him up the single flight of stairs and into a ward comprised of cubicles. In one of these was the doomed woman, her head swathed in bandages, and the visible portion of the face looking like old ivory. The eyelids flickered a little as the doctor reached out and felt her pulse. He turned to McLean.

'It's now or never,' he whispered. 'You can try.'

McLean came forward, and leaned close to the woman.

'Mrs. Trapping. I am a police officer. Can you hear me?'

The eyes opened a little wider and stared at him.

'Can you tell me who did this to you?'

The bloodless lips moved a little, and McLean strained his ears to catch the tiniest whisper.

'It – it was my – my—'

'Go on,' he murmured.

But the head jerked suddenly. There was a little plaintive sigh, and then silence.

'All over,' said the doctor. 'What did she say?'

'Nothing very definite. I suppose she has made no other statement of any kind since she has been here?'

'None. She has been unconscious all the time.'

McLean went outside where he had left Sergeant Brook in the police car.

'Any luck, sir?' Brook asked.

'She's dead. She tried to tell me who it was who struck her down. But all she could say was "It was my—" Then death sealed her lips.'

'But it helps a bit doesn't it? I mean it was obviously someone close to her.'

'Yes, but think how many persons it could apply to. Her brother, son, cousin, son-in-law—'

'Has she got all those relatives—'

'I don't know since the circumstances took me straight to the hospital. Drive me to County Police Headquarters, and we'll see what the position is.'

At County Police Headquarters McLean and Brook saw the officer who had had charge of the case. His name was Inspector Flower, and he seemed a little hurt that he had not been permitted to follow up the preliminary inquiry.

'She was found in a dying state by George Warren, the cowman at Lockwood Farm at seven o'clock last evening, and we were advised immediately. The body was lying half in a ditch in Sandy Lane, about half a mile from the farmhouse. It was dark when we arrived and we were not able to make a thorough investigation of the site. But there is another lane leading to the farm, so I closed Sandy Lane, by posting a man at either end, and informed the farmer that it was out of use.'

'Good!' said McLean. 'Now tell me what you know about the victim.'

'She is fifty-three years of age, and lives – or lived – at Rose Cottage – a white house about two hundred yards from where her body was found. Until three years ago she lived with her husband, who was employed at a big grain merchants in the town. Then he died, leaving her very little, and she got a job as cashier in the firm which had employed her husband.'

'What is the name of the firm?'

'Bulton Brothers – in South Street.'

'Was she happy there?'

'Yes. I saw the senior partner. He said she was very competent, and they were glad to have been able to employ her. Yesterday she left the office at the usual time – five-thirty. There was time for her to catch the five-forty bus to Yapton. That's the bus stop quite near the end of Sandy Lane, where she should have arrived at five minutes past six. From there to the spot where the body was found is only ten minutes' walk. But the doctor's opinion was that she had been struck down only a few minutes before Warren found her. So there is a time gap, not yet explained.'

'You are only assuming she caught that bus?'

'Yes. But the next bus to Yapton is an hour later, so that won't meet the case.'

'She could have missed the first bus, and got a lift in a car.'

'Yes, of course.'

'Did she live alone?'

'No. She had a paying guest to help her finances. I haven't seen him yet, because he was away when I visited the cottage.'

'What about relatives?'

'A married daughter living out at Rogate, and a son who is believed to be in Leeds.'

'He would be the next of kin?'

'Yes.'

'Have you communicated with the daughter?'

'Yes. She rang up the hospital but they wouldn't permit her to see her mother.'

'And the son?'

'An inquiry has gone through to Leeds, but so far there has been no reply.'

II

McLean and Brook then went to the scene of the crime, equipped with powerful electric lamps. They were stopped at the entrance to the narrow lane by the officer on duty there. McLean produced his warrant, and they proceeded and were soon on the actual site indicated by two white pegs driven into the grass verge. Here they searched for about half an hour in the hope of finding a clue of some sort, but all they found was scattered blood, and a pool of it where the woman had lain.

'We'll have to come again in daylight,' said McLean. 'Let's go on to the cottage.'

It was only a few seconds before McLean saw the white cottage loom up. To his surprise there were lights in the windows. The car was stopped outside the cottage, and McLean and Brook went to the door. A ring of the bell brought a middle-aged man to the door. He quizzed them suspiciously.

'We are police officers,' said McLean. 'Do you live here?'

'I lodge here. My name is Michael Watson. If you want Mrs. Trapping I think she's in bed. I've only been here a few minutes.'

'How did you get here without being stopped?' asked McLean.

'Stopped? Why should I be stopped?'

'The lane has been closed for hours.'

'I didn't come down the lane. I caught the last bus from the town, but it stops short of Yapton, and from where I got off it is quicker by the field paths. There is one right at the back of the cottage. Why is the lane closed?'

'Mrs. Trapping was murdered in the lane earlier this evening.'

'Good heavens! How shocking! But please come in. I – I thought she had gone to bed. She often did that when I was out late.'

He led them to a small sitting-room, where McLean saw his hat and coat lying across a chair.

'When did you last see Mrs. Tapping?' McLean asked.

'This morning. We both went to business on the same bus. I'm a clerk at the brewery. I only have bed and breakfast here as Mrs. Trapping was away all day.'

'Do you know any reason why Mrs. Trapping should be attacked?'

'No. She was a very kind and charming woman.'

'How long have you been lodging here?'

'Nearly three years. I came a few months after her husband died.'

'Have you met her son?'

'No. She has spoken of him, but I've never seen him.'

'Do you know where he can be found?'

'No, but I think she told me he was a motor engineer in Leeds.'

McLean then went over the house with Brook. It was a well-built place with four bedrooms and bathroom, and equipped with all main services and telephone. Everything was scrupulously clean and tidy, and in the dead woman's bedroom the bed was made, and her clothing neatly arranged in wardrobe and chests. A bureau yielded a few things of interest. She had war saving certificates to the value of a thousand pounds, all of which had matured, and in a Post Office savings book there was a credit balance of £320. There were some letters from her married daughter, all very friendly and happy, and one letter dated a month previously from her son, Joseph.

This threw no light on the matter, but is gave the son's address, which was Bradford, and not Leeds as had been stated. He mentioned the fact that he had changed his lodgings, as he had been transferred to the Bradford branch of the firm he worked for.

'He's on the telephone,' said McLean. 'We'll try and get him in a few minutes.'

Later, when McLean had decided to postpone further investigation until the next morning, Joseph Trapping was rung up. The bell rang for a long time before there came an answer in a sleepy voice.

'Are you Mr. Trapping?' asked McLean.

'No, I'm the owner of the house. Mr. Trapping lodges here, but went to bed half an hour ago. Can I take a message?'

'I should prefer to speak to Mr. Trapping.'

'All right. Hang on please. Oh, what name?'

'It doesn't matter, but tell him it is very important, and concerns his mother.'

Then came Trapping's anxious voice. McLean told him the bad news, and heard his little gasp of horror. Finally it was arranged that McLean should meet him at his mother's house the next morning at eleven o'clock.

'If he was in bed half an hour ago that seems to give him a clean bill,' said Brook. 'He couldn't have got back to Bradford in the time.'

'No, I think he couldn't. But his evidence may be useful.'

'What about the lodger here?'

'I'm wondering about him,' replied McLean. 'It's his name that sticks in my gills.'

'Michael Watson,' muttered Brook. 'But why?'

'The first syllable, Brook. I told you what the dying woman said.'

Brook thought for a moment, and then gave a start.

'My goodness!' he ejaculated. 'She might have been going to say "Michael" not "my" something or other. That's pretty queer, isn't it?'

'It's still only an assumption. On the face of it he had nothing to gain by the death of his landlady. We must make some more inquiries in that direction. But not tonight. We'll see him early in the morning.'

McLean and Brook slept in the nearby town that night, but early the next morning they were on the trail again. A very concentrated search was made near the spot where the body was found, and in the ditch in dense long grass a small plated electric torch was found. McLean handled it with the utmost care.

'Mrs. Trapping's or her murderer's?' he asked.

'Or neither?' put in Brook.

'Yes, or neither. I want this taken to the laboratory at once, then we'll run out to Rogate and see the dead woman's sister. Her married name is Hilditch.'

The torch was taken to Police headquarters, and a very quick and excellent job was done on it by the fingerprint department. Within an hour McLean had a dried print, showing three fingers and thumb of a left hand.

'Obviously the murderer held his bludgeon in his right hand,' he mused. 'The woman, I think, put up some resistance, causing him to drop the torch. Now we'll go to Rogate.'

But this trip was rendered unnecessary by the sudden appearance of Mrs. Hilditch and her husband at the police station. They had heard from the hospital that Mrs. Trapping was dead. Mrs. Hilditch was in tears, but her husband had complete control of himself. In reply to McLean's questions they said that they had not seen the dead woman for over a month, and they knew of no reason why she should be attacked. They were together the whole of the previous evening at their home. McLean, to save time, asked them if they were willing to have their fingerprints taken, and they said they were. The result exonerated them so far as the torch was concerned.

McLean and Brook then motored to Rose Cottage, where they found the lodger getting ready to go to business. Watson was questioned about his movements the preceding evening, and gave what appeared to be a first-class alibi. McLean again suggested fingerprints, and Watson was quite agreeable. They took him to police headquarters, and the result was the same as with the Hilditches.

'Can it be that the torch had nothing to do with the murder?' asked Brook.

'I don't think so. A very small spot of blood was found on the bottom of it. But I'm going to have the dead woman's fingers examined, to settle that point.'

But it was the same with the victim as with the suspects, and McLean's hopes rose again. He and Brook managed to get to Rose Cottage in time to receive the son. His alibi was perfect, for by no means could he have done the murder and got to Bradford in the time permitted.

'I have not seen my mother for a long time,' he said. 'But I heard from her occasionally. When my father died I offered to make her a weekly allowance, but she was very independent and told me she could manage quite well, by getting a job and taking a lodger. I gathered that she was quite satisfied with Mr. Watson. I can't understand this cruel murder. It seems quite senseless, and yet someone must have stood to gain from it.'

McLean was quite certain about that, but now he had to look outside Mrs. Trapping's immediate circle. He found the conductor of the five-forty bus to Yapton on the evening of the crime. She was a woman, and knew Mrs. Trapping well by sight. She said that Mrs. Trapping had not been on the bus that evening·

'Just what we expected,' said McLean to Brook. 'It looks very much as if someone in a car gave her a lift as far as the end of Sandy Lane. Even so there is still a time gap. My guess is that she met somebody she knew, after she had left the car, and walked down the lane with him.'

'Someone who knew she nearly always caught that bus and was waiting for her?'

'Yes. They could have used up time in conversation, or argument. Then at a favourable spot she was savagely attacked and left for dead. We shall have to make a further search in Rose Cottage.'

The two police sentries had now been removed, and McLean and Brook reached the cottage without interception. McLean opened up the place and started a most meticulous search. It looked as if Mrs. Trapping had feared burglars, for under the mattress of her bed there was a thin flat box, containing her marriage certificate, a will made in favour of her two children in equal portions, some odd pieces of jewellery, and a document in a long envelope. McLean drew out the document. It was a lease of the house dating back twenty years, on an annual basis, at forty pounds per annum, and signed by John Trapping, and one Edward Dodge, of Shortlands, Yapton.

'So she was only a tenant here,' mused McLean. 'I think we might do worse than run along to Shortlands, but where is it?'

'Shall we try the farm first. They are bound to know.'

McLean was agreeable, but as they went to the car George Warren, the cowman who had made the discovery, came down the lane driving a couple of heifers. McLean stopped him.

'Do you know a Mr. Dodge of Shortlands,' he asked.

'Aye, but Shortlands ain't Shortlands any longer. After Mr. Edward died his widow sold it and turned it into flats. It's along the main road about a mile.'

'Does this cottage belong to Mrs. Dodge?'

'No. She inherited the big house and some land, but the son Peter was left Rose Cottage.'

'Where can I find him?'

'I dunno. The last time I saw him was a month ago when he was seeing Mrs. Trapping about some repairs she wanted done to the roof. But she didn't get 'em done, as I knew she wouldn't.'

'How did you know?'

'A matter of cost I reckon. I know Peter hasn't got any money, and a new roof costs a lot. Can't even raise money on property these days when you've got a sitting tenant.'

That phrase rang in McLean's ears as he entered the car, and told Brook to drive back to the town. There McLean found out where Peter Dodge was living, and learned quite a lot of things about him. He had inherited a good sum of money along with Rose Cottage, but had gambled it away. There was evidence in a solicitors office that he had tried unsuccessfully to sell Rose Cottage to its tenant, and further evidence that he had actually raised a small sum on it from a bank, which was pressing him for repayment. Now he himself was living in one room of a small house in the worst part of the town.

'Would it surprise you, Brook, if I suggested the word

94

which poor Mrs. Trapping was trying to utter with her last breath?' he asked.

'Could it be "landlord",' asked Brook.

'I think it could. But let's put it to the test.'

But when McLean called at the house where Dodge was lodging he was informed that Dodge had gone on a journey. The woman who kept the house didn't know where.

'When did he leave here?' asked McLean.

'On Wednesday night, about half past eight. He was here until five o'clock and then left and came back at eight. I thought he looked ill, and told him so. He said he had just had some bad news and had to go at once to London.'

'Did he say when he would be back?'

'He said in a few days.'

'Have you ever seen a small electric torch in his room, with an octagonal top and a ring at the bottom, electroplated all over?'

'Yes, often.'

'Will you see if it is in his room now?'

The woman went upstairs and after some time came down to say the torch didn't appear to be there.

'Thank you!' said McLean. 'If Mr. Dodge should come back I want you to telephone to this number without delay, and without informing him. Will you do that?'

'Y-yes,' she stammered.

But the telephone message did not come, and McLean got a detailed description of Peter Dodge, and used the B.B.C. An hour after the message was put out a man rang up from a lodging house in Hoxton. He said that a man answering the description, but who had given another name, was in the bedroom he had rented, and in a drunken sleep.

'This is it,' said McLean. 'Let's go.'

Later they found Dodge recovering from his drunken orgy. All his answers to McLean's questions were most unsatisfactory, and finally he was taken to Scotland Yard. Within a few minutes the fingerprints on the torch were found to be his. He was formally charged with murder.

10

L ONDON and the home counties were suffering from yet
another of their periodical crime waves. Within a period
of just over a month there had been five robberies in
country houses, and in every case the thieves had got
away with valuable booty. The evidence pointed to a
well-organized and well-equipped gang, for where burglar
alarms were installed these were located in advance and
cleverly put out of action. In one house a watch-dog had
been drugged with a hunk of doped meat, and the burglars seemed to have an uncanny knowledge of hidden
safes, and employed what appeared to be a new type of
steel drill to cut away the lock.

McLean had investigated no less than four of these
cases with no success. They were not confined to any
particular district, and it was thus quite impossible to
put on enough extra night patrols to deal with the situation. There was little doubt that a car was being used,
and a large number of police cars equipped with wireless were on the roads every night, on the alert for any
message which might announce a new robbery.

'They're cute,' said Sergeant Brook. 'Here we've a list
of stolen articles big enough to make a book, and not
a single one of them has been traced. Looks as though
there's a hoard somewhere.'

'Did you try Bridger?'

Bridger was an ex-fence, now in the pay of the police.
He knew all the ramifications of the trade in stolen
property, and could by examining lists give a pretty
good idea of the destination of particular articles.

'Bridger says they're not in the market,' replied Brook.
'He went to Amsterdam as suggested, but couldn't get a
line on anything. Take that big ruby for example – the
one pinched from Aldburgh Park. Bridger says no one
would handle it as it was, and that it would have to be
sliced up. He says he has seen the only men who could do
the cutting, and he's quite certain they know nothing
about it.'

'Do you think Bridger is reliable?'

'That's what I've been wondering. He certainly did

good work for us when he first came over, but if anyone else has got hold of him I wouldn't like to say he wouldn't double cross us.'

Two days after this conversation took place an urgent telephone message was received during the night. It informed the police that a robbery had taken place at Fox's Farm near Weybridge, and that the thieves had only just got away. McLean was awakened from sleep. The car patrol was immediately informed by wireless, and in a very short time McLean and Brook in a wireless-equipped car were speeding through the night towards the scene of the robbery.

'Quick warning this time,' said Brook. 'We ought to be able to do something. Four of the patrol cars were quite nicely disposed when the SOS came.'

A little later they drew up beside one of the patrol cars which had taken up a position at some cross roads. McLean spoke to the officer in charge.

'Nothing has passed here, sir,' he said. 'Except a man on a motor cycle. I satisfied myself that he was all right.'

'Better stay here until you receive further instructions,' McLean spoke to the officer in charge.

As they drew near Fox's Farm another police car was encountered and here again there was no useful information. As McLean now had control of the road leading to the farm the car was posted to another spot, and Brook drove on.

Fox's Farm was a reconstructed farmhouse, of the kind sought after by well-to-do persons, who usually do no farming, but like to feel they are on the land. Illuminated by the headlights of the car it looked very attractive, for all the old timbers had been retained and freshly treated, and the garden in front of it had been nicely laid out. All the lights in the house were full on when McLean rang the bell. A scared-looking maidservant opened the door, and peered at him.

'The police?' she quavered.

'Yes.'

'Oh, please come in. Her ladyship's been so anxious.'

At that moment Lady Frederica Moreton appeared from a room on the right of the hall. She was a big impressive sort of woman, and at this moment she looked very aggressive.

'Scotland Yard,' she said, as she perused the card which the girl had given her. 'But I telephoned the local police.'

'We are working with the County police in the matter of these robberies,' said McLean.

'I'm so glad, Inspector. Please come in here.'

She led McLean and Brook into the lovely lounge, which was furnished in excellent taste. But now there were several pictures on the floor, and in the wall on the right side of the fireplace was an exposed safe. The floor was littered with metal, and McLean on going closer saw that the door of the safe had been drilled all round the lock, so thoroughly as to allow the whole lock to be removed. The interior of the safe was disorderly, and on the long table he saw a metal box which had been broken open. It was now empty.

'All my jewellery,' said her ladyship. I never dreamed it could happen to me. No one in this house even knew I had a safe, because I had it installed when I bought the house two years ago, and had that very heavy picture hung over it.'

'Tell me exactly what happened. How did you discover that the house was being burgled?'

'Just luck. Fort he past few days I've been suffering from dental trouble. I had a tooth extracted yesterday, and all last evening I had toothache – jaw-ache to be correct. I went to bed early, but woke at intervals with gnawing pain. It was a quarter past two when I woke up with the same nasty pain. I thought that perhaps a couple of aspirins would settle my nerves, and got out of bed to get them. It was then I heard a noise from downstairs. It was certainly metallic, and seemed to come from directly underneath me – from this room. There was only Helen – the maid – in the house. Both the cook and gardener come daily. But I'm not a very nervous woman and I decided to bluff it out if I could. I had my husband's old army revolver in a drawer, but there was no ammunition. Still, I thought it might scare any burglar away. So I crept downstairs. It was all in darkness below, but when I listened outside this door I could hear very slight noises. Suddenly I pushed the door open and switched on the light. Two men were standing by the table, one with a torch in his hand. The other one was emptying my jewellery from the metal box into a small bag. I raised the revolver, and told him to put it down. To my horror he produced a pistol, and completely turned the tables on me. He told me to stand away from the door, or he would shoot. I – I lost my nerve, knowing that the revolver was useless. I stood aside and they passed me and went out by the door. Then I remembered the telephone, and rushed to it. I couldn't get on to the exchange, and a moment or two later I saw that the wire had been cut. I put on a coat and ran to the next door house. It took some minutes to rouse Mr. Martin. From there I telephoned the police station.'

McLean went to the telephone which was in the room and saw that the cable had been cut through, in such a way that it was not immediately obvious to anyone using the instrument.

'What were the two men like?' he asked.

'One of them was quite old – fifty at least. He was the man who produced the pistol. He had a hat on and dark overcoat. Clean-shaven and a square type of face – much lined. His confederate was much younger – about thirty. He was thin and very tall, with a slight dark moustache. He never spoke a word all the time. He was very round shouldered – and almost stooped as he walked.'

'Did you hear the sound of a car after they had left?'

'No. Nothing at all.'

'Have you discovered how they gained entry to the house?'

'Yes – through the window of the downstairs toilet. That window was left open, but it's so small I shouldn't have thought it possible for anyone to get through. But outside the window there is a flower bed. The man who entered brought some fresh earth with him. I'll show you.'

She led them along the hall and entered a small toilet room at the end of it. When she switched on the light McLean could see the fresh soil left on the light-coloured floor-covering.

'I'm certain the older man couldn't have got through,' said her ladyship. 'I think the smaller man must have opened the front door to him.'

'Have you looked outside this window?'

'No.'

McLean left the house and walked round the corner

of it until he came to the flower bed under the window of the toilet room. There was a disturbance of the earth but no footprints.

'The big man had the sense to cover them up,' said Brook.

'It certainly looks like it. Well, let's see what we can discover inside the house.'

II

McLean, on re-entering the house, asked Lady Moreton to be good enough to make a full list of the stolen articles, and while this was being done he made a thorough search for fingerprints. But there wasn't a sign of any. He examined the ruined door of the safe, and saw that much oil had been used in the drilling to reduce the noise of the drill.

'A very good job indeed,' he said. 'They must have taken over an hour to make all those holes, and even then the drill used must have been of exceptional quality.'

'Just like the others,' said Brook.

'Yes. I think there's no doubt that it is the work of the same gang. Shall I try to repair this telephone wire?'

'Do. I should like to get through to London.'

Brook made quite a good job of the repair in a short time, and McLean then telephoned headquarters, and asked if there was any news from the various patrols.

'No luck,' he said, as he hung up the receiver. 'If a car was used it got clean away.'

'Not surprising,' said Brook. 'We'd need thirty cars to control all roads in this neighbourhood. Well, this job is number six of the series, and there's no guarantee that it will be the last.'

Lady Moreton was not long in producing her list of stolen jewellery. There were some twenty articles in all, and by the side of each item was its insured value.

'Six thousand pounds in all,' said McLean, as he totalled up the items. 'Quite a nice haul. Are you quite sure that nobody here knew about the existence of the safe?'

'Not unless it was found accidentally.'

'But what happens when you place things in it?'

'I always lock the door of the room.'

'But how do you get to the safe, if it's behind the heavy picture?'

'It's quite possible to swing the picture aside. But nobody would be likely to move it to any extent in the process of dusting.'

McLean looked towards the large french windows.

'You might be seen from the garden,' he suggested.

'I doubt it. In any case the gardener is a very trustworthy person. He's been with me for many years. I even brought him with me from my last house two years ago.'

'And the maidservant?'

'She's very stupid – too stupid to be anything but honest.'

'I think I'd like to question her. She may have met some nice young man, and talked a lot.'

'I'll send her in,' said her ladyship, 'but I don't think she'll help much.'

When the girl entered she looked very nervous, and sat down in the chair which McLean offered as if she expected there was a bomb under it.

'What's your name?' asked McLean.

'Helen Hexter.'

'How long have you been in Lady Moreton's employ?'

'Just over two years, sir.'

'Have you a boy friend?'

'Eh?' she asked blankly.

'A regular young man who takes you out?'

'I did have once,' she said sadly. 'But he borrowed some money and ran away.'

Brook smiled but McLean remained quite serious. He pointed to the open safe.

'Did you know there was a safe under that picture?' he asked.

'Oh no,' she said. 'Not until tonight when the mistress came and woke me up and told me she had been robbed. When I came downstairs she showed me what had happened.'

'And you had no idea your mistress kept her jewellery in that safe?'

'No. I thought she kept it in her bedroom somewhere.'

'Have there been any strange callers here recently?'

'Quite a lot. We're always getting men at the door trying to sell things like Hoovers and water softeners. Sometimes they try to sell me a watch or stockings at the back door, but the mistress told me I wasn't to encourage men like that, so I don't.'

'Have you ever mentioned your mistress's jewellery to anyone at all?'

'Oh no – I mean not to anyone outside the house. Cook and me have mentioned it perhaps once or twice when the mistress wore it.'

'Was the cook here when you first came?'

'Yes. She was with the mistress at her last house. You see, she's the wife of the gardener. They agreed to come with the mistress, and they live in a cottage just down the lane, and they come in daily.'

McLean dismissed her, and then he and Brook made a thorough examination of the ground outside the house, between the window of entry and the entrance gate to the drive. Nothing was found which helped the case to any degree. They re-entered the house, and spent some time on the actual scene of the crime.

'A complete blank,' said Brook.

McLean had turned out the waste-paper basket, and in this, among other things, he found a piece of the flexible telephone-wire casing which Brook had stripped off from the broken wire before making his repair.

'Very interesting,' he said.

'What?' asked Brook.

'This piece of casing. I think before we go we'll have a look round the house – and that includes all the rooms.'

'But doesn't the evidence show that the burglars came straight in here?' asked Brook.

'Yes, but we'll look round all the same.'

Her ladyship had no objection, and room after room was very closely examined. When McLean had finished downstairs he went upstairs. Her ladyship's room showed a disturbed bed. Apart from her scattered clothing everything else was tidy. McLean pryed into everything, and then went to the only other bedroom which had been occupied – that of Helen the maidservant. It was almost as nice a room as that of the mistress of the house. Here again the bed was disturbed. Near the window was the 'dummy' model of a woman, with a garment stretched over it. It was an unfinished outdoor coat, and was very stylish.

'Helen isn't so stupid if she made that,' said McLean.

The girl then came into the room.

'Oh!' she gasped. 'I didn't know—'

'It's all right,' said McLean. 'I was wondering whether the burglars might have come up here while you were sleeping. So you're a dressmaker?'

'Yes,' she said. 'My mother was a professional, but a girl can't make a living that way these days.'

In a corner McLean saw a workbasket. It was full of wools and cottons. Brook saw a flash of bright metal and then realized that McLean had slipped something into his pocket.

'All right,' he said. 'I expect you want to get to bed, Miss Hexter. There's nothing here of any importance.'

At the foot of the stairs he met Lady Moreton.

'They seem to have confined their activities to downstairs,' he said. 'I don't propose to do any more tonight. You had better telephone your insurance company the first thing in the morning. In the meantime we shall circulate descriptions of the missing articles.'

'Thank you, Inspector,' she said. 'I'll see you to the door. Poor Helen is dead tired, and rather scared.'

'Oh, please don't bother.'

'No bother at all.'

At the door McLean thanked her, and said he would be back in the morning. Then he suddenly remembered something.

'Where were you living before you came here?' he asked.

'Broadbent Manor in Derbyshire. Broadbent is just a small village. I wanted to get south – nearer London.'

'I don't blame you,' said McLean. 'Well, good night Lady Moreton.'

III

McLean got little sleep that night, for he had business with the Derbyshire police, and that meant hours at the telephone while inquiries went forward. At last he got what was immediately necessary and referred to his writing pad.

'Her full name is Lady Patricia Frederica Moreton,

and she is the widow of Sir Alfred Moreton, who died four years ago. Before her marriage she was a show-girl.'

'Phew!' whistled Brook.

'Nothing very unusual in that,' said McLean. 'When an old man marries a comparatively young girl he is usually attracted by the glamorous type. Well, Moreton died leaving nothing worth mentioning except a large house. Lady Moreton continued to live there for two years and then managed to sell the place, and bought her present much smaller residence. The Derbyshire police cannot discover that any servants from Broadbent Manor came south with Lady Moreton, and they believe that she was abroad for six months before she moved south. But I shall know more on that point tomorrow.'

'So you think this is a racket?' said Brook.

'I do. Lady Moreton has a right to use that title, but I mistrusted the maid the moment I saw her. That look of stupidity isn't genuine. Her hands were in perfect condition, and her dressing-table was loaded down with cosmetics. But that isn't all. It was your telephone repair which provided a very important clue. This.'

McLean produced from his pocket the small piece of telephone-wire casing which he had found in the waste-paper basket. He showed it to Brook, and for a moment Brook saw nothing interesting in it.

'Look at that mark on the casing – just above the place where you used the pliers to cut off this end piece.'

Brook looked and saw a curious zig-zag mark across the casing.

'What is it?' he asked.

'It was the result of an attempt to cut the wire with an instrument not intended to cut wire. I was reminded of a similar tool which I've often seen my mother use in dressmaking. Ever heard of pinking scissors?'

'Never.'

'This is where I improve your education. These, my dear Brook, are pinking scissors.'

He produced a pair of very large scissors which when closed looked exactly like the usual kind, but on opening the blades Brook saw that both edges were serrated. He cut the edge of a newspaper and produced a beautifully regular serrated edge.

'Clever,' he said. 'What are they used for?'

'Hems of garments. Tonight they were used for a different purpose.'

'To cut the telephone cable?'

'Yes. It wasn't successful, and so I presume a better tool was used. Had I found the scissors in that room I might have thought the burglars were responsible, but they were in the maid's room. I'm certain it was she who cut the telephone wire or, at least, who tried to cut it with these scissors.'

'Looks absolutely conclusive,' agreed Brook. 'It's a fake and Lady Moreton must be in the swindle.'

'Very much in it.'

'But it bore all the signs of the old gang—'

'I am convinced she is the old gang.'

'By jove – what a nerve!'

'Yes, she has plenty of nerve. It was a bold thing to do, but there was a certain amount of logic in it. She stands to gain six thousand pounds from the insurance company, and at the same time she gives us an entirely wrong description of the persons we are after. The whole thing was cleverly done. The one mistake was the silly attempt on the telephone cable with these scissors, and that was probably the girl's blunder. I credit the other persons with more sense.'

'Persons! That includes the gardener and his wife?'

'Yes. It required a man to drill all those holes in the safe door – a man with considerable engineering skill. Well, let's see what tomorrow will bring. We shall only get about four hours' sleep.'

.   .   .   .   .

Early the following morning McLean was informed over the telephone that all the servants employed at Lady Moreton's last house were accounted for. Not one of them had gone with her to the new place.

'That seems to clear up things,' said McLean. 'She must have met those people abroad, and have joined their racket. Her title would help things considerably. I'm going to arrest the whole lot. We shall need an extra car.'

But McLean had underestimated the intelligence of the gang. When the two police cars arrived at the farm the house was unoccupied. The car had gone, and there were signs of a hasty departure, but the expensive furniture remained.

'They must have discovered the loss of the scissors, and when I inquired about the last address of Lady Moreton I think she feared the result of our investigations. We've got to get busy, or they will leave the country.'

A little later all the ports in Great Britain were advised to look out for the four persons involved, and McLean rather regretted that he hadn't made the acquaintance of the gardener and cook before he had left the house the previous night, for the only detailed descriptions he could give were those of Lady Moreton and Helen Hexter. But he had taken the registration number of the car they had used, and this he hoped would help.

It did help, for six hours later the abandoned car was found not far from Exeter. McLean consulted the map, and realized that the place where the car was found was some distance from the city, but in a favourable place for the occupants to get to the airport from which there was a service to the Channel Islands.

'It would just suit them,' he said. 'Probably they were cute enough to realize that they couldn't get to a foreign country because of their passports, which would give away their names. But no passport is required for the Channel Islands.'

He used the telephone, the line of which was being 'held', and requested the Exeter police to make inquiries at the airport, and to report back as quickly as possible. Half an hour later the Exeter police were on the line again. They had been to the airport and had detained four persons who had been about to take the air liner to Jersey. They all gave names different from those which McLean had given, but the two younger women answered the descriptions.

'Hold them,' said McLean. 'I'm coming down.'

An airplane was requisitioned, and a little later Brook and McLean were flying over the sunlit countryside at close on two hundred miles an hour. For the last hundred miles the sea was visible all the time, and in due course they landed at the airport. McLean met the local officer on leaving the plane.

'I've got them, Inspector,' he said. 'I found the man trying to dispose of this, while I wasn't looking. Just caught him in time.'

He handed McLean a very strongly made attaché-case. It had two locks and was fairly heavy.

'Locked,' said the officer. 'I thought I'd better leave it for you.'

McLean nodded and took over the case. He was then conducted to a private room in the airport, and on the door being opened by a uniformed police officer McLean saw the big frame of Lady Moreton, and beside her her late 'maidservant' and a grizzled man and woman. The 'maidservant' looked very different now, for she was wearing a very nice costume and the latest things in hats. Lady Moreton's nerve gave way when she realized there was no way out.

'Have you the key to this case?' asked McLean.

'He – he has it,' she said, indicating the grizzled man.

McLean turned to the man, gave him a long look, and then swiftly turned back the cuff of his right sleeve. High up on the wrist he saw a long scar.

'We're in luck,' he said. 'Henri Colbert, whom the French police have been looking for. Expert safe-cracker and other things. Come on M'sieur – the key.'

The savage-looking man didn't attempt to deny the accusation. He produced a small key and the attaché-case was opened. It was full to the brim with jewellery, among which McLean recognized a number of articles from descriptions provided by the real owners, and among these was the big valuable ruby.

In London Lady Moreton made a full confession. Colbert was the brains behind the racket. She had met him in Monte Carlo, where she had lost the money she had got from the sale of the old house, and he, after getting to know her desperate straits, had put up a proposition. It was Colbert who had bought the farm in her name, and who had planned all the robberies. The burgling of his own house was to be the last. After that there was to be a share-out of the proceeds of two years' work, and they were going to part company. The woman who had passed herself off as cook was not his wife but his sister. Helen Hexter was an old stage associate of Lady Moreton's before she married.

'I've been silly,' she said, wiping away a tear. 'But I can't think how you came to suspect us.'

'Didn't you discover the loss of the pinking scissors?' asked McLean.

'What pinking scissors?' she asked.

Helen looked very shamefaced, and McLean turned to Colbert.

'You must have known,' he said.

Colbert shrugged his shoulders.

'It is a lesson to me,' he said. 'No expert should work with amateurs. These two women are not capable of learning anything at all.'

'I'm rather hoping they've learnt that crime doesn't pay,' replied McLean. 'That goes for you too, Colbert.'

Colbert laughed in a high rasping cackle.

11

DESPITE the instructions given him over the telephone Inspector McLean hád some difficulty in finding Bracken-side House, for it lay in a stretch of heathland, a long way from any semblance of a road, some twenty miles south of London, and was approachable only by a rough cart-track. But at last, in pitch darkness, the headlights of the car revealed an old notice-board bearing the name in faded white lettering.

'At last!' sighed Sergeant Brook, who was driving the police car. 'What a place to live in!'

The house soon came into view. It was a grim-looking place enclosed in a natural garden of woodland and fern, and in the drizzling rain its dilapidations looked all the more depressing. McLean got out of the car and hurried to the front door, for the matter was of great urgency.

'White elephant,' muttered Brook, as McLean pushed the bell. 'Hasn't been painted in twenty years. An oil lamp too in these days.'

The door was opened by a man of about fifty years of age, with a pallid face and frightened eyes.

'The police?' he asked.

'Yes,' replied McLean. 'Are you Mr. Waller, who made the telephone call?'

'Yes. I had to walk a mile to do that. Something dreadful has happened here—'

'I know,' said McLean, cutting him short· 'Take me to Mr. Rossiter.'

Mr. Waller gulped and led them into a barely furnished hall, which was dimly lighted by another oil lamp. He opened a door on the right.

'He – he's in there,' he quavered.

McLean and Brook stepped into a large room, where yet another oil lamp was burning. A huge log was smouldering in an old-fashioned open fireplace, and between this and an oval mahogany table lay the form of an old man, with his body curled up and blood all over his neck and head.

'Is this all the light we can get?' asked McLean.

'Yes, sir. There are no main services here. The master was going to have electricity brought in, but—'

McLean leaned over the corpse. He had been struck one or two heavy blows on the head, and the hands were already stone cold. On the floor quite near the body was a heavy silver candlestick, and two red candles which had fallen from it. On the base of the candlestick was blood.

'Hey, there's a pistol near the couch,' said Brook.

'I know,' said McLean. 'Leave it for a moment. Now, Mr. Waller, what do you know about this?'

'Nothing, sir. It was my evening off, and at six o'clock I came in here to tell Mr. Rossiter I was about to leave, and ask if he needed anything. He told me to bring the candlestick to the table as he wanted to read. I did this and lighted the candles. Then I left.'

'When did you get back?'

'At a quarter past ten. My bus reached Paston's corner at ten o'clock. I had to walk from there.'

'Did you see anybody near the house when you left at six o'clock?'

'No. But a car passed me just before I got to the busstop. It was coming this way. But it could have been going to Winterfold, for that track serves both houses.'

'Did you see who was in the car?'

'It was very dark, but I think there were two men – in the front seat.'

'What make of car?'

'A Vauxhall. Mr. Rossiter has one of the same make.
But ours is black and the other was grey.'
'How long have you been with Mr. Rossiter?'
'Just over six years.'
'Are there no other persons in the house?'
'No. There is a woman who cycles here every morning
from Ewell, but she leaves after lunch is cleared away.'
'Was Mr. Rossiter engaged in any profession?'
'Oh no. He was a retired gentleman. I think he was
a civil servant or something like that before his retire-
ment. A very quiet gentleman. Spent most of his time
reading.'
'Any relatives?'
'I think he has a son abroad, because I've posted letters
to a Mr. John Rossiter, at an address in Paris.'
'Can you remember the exact address?'
Mr. Waller reflected for a moment.
'It was either 26 or 36 Rue de Chartres.'
'Have you established if there is anything missing from
the house?'
'Yes, sir. There is nothing missing so far as I can
discover.'
'And that pistol on the floor—have you ever seen it
before?'
'I think so, sir. There was one like it in the drawer
under that table.'
McLean went to the table and opened the drawer.
There was no pistol inside. He stepped across to the
pistol on the floor and handled it carefully by the end of
the barrel. He slipped out the magazine and found eight
cartridges in it.
'Fully loaded,' he mused. 'Mr. Waller, did Mr. Rossiter
ever tell you why he kept a loaded weapon in that
drawer?'
'No, sir. But this is a very lonely spot, and I suppose he
was nervous of burglars.'
'Where was the candlestick before you brought it to
the table?' asked McLean.
'On the mantelpiece.'
'That's all for the moment, Mr. Waller.'
Waller left the room, and McLean picked up the
candlestick with a silk handkerchief, also the red candles.
'There's no doubt he was killed by a blow from the

heavy base,' he said. 'It may yield fingerprints, but I doubt very much whether the murderer would overlook those. The pistol was never fired. It was knocked from his hand before he could press the trigger. Oh, one moment! '

He went to the corpse, and pulled back the sleeves of the coat. On the right wrist was an injury, just above the face of a gold wrist-watch, the glass of which was shattered.

'Yes – there's the evidence,' he said. 'Gives us the time of the attack, if we can trust he watch. It stopped at seven-twenty-six.'

II

On McLean's orders Brook drove into the nearby town, and came back with an ambulance and a police surgeon. The latter kept the ambulance waiting while he made some tests.

'Dead several hours,' he said. 'Impossible to give any exact time. Depends upon so many factors. I would say four hours at least.'

'Would he have survived his injuries for any length of time?'

'Half an hour perhaps. Do you want him any longer?'

'No. I've been through the clothing.'

The body was removed and McLean then examined the articles taken from the clothing. Amongst them was a letter from the son whom Waller had mentioned. It gave his full address and his telephone number in Paris, and was dated three days previously.

'Just an ordinary letter,' said McLean. 'Wants to know why his father stays in this ruin when he can easily afford to buy a decent small house.'

'Are those his keys?' asked Brook, pointing to half a dozen small keys on a ring.

'Yes. I want to check those. One is presumably the front door key, and I think two of the others are for the garage and car. That still leaves two others. We'll have a look at the garage now.'

They went outside and opened up the place.. A black Vauxhall saloon car stood inside. It looked as if it had not been used for several days, as there was a fine coating of dust on it. McLean locked the door again and searched the ground for signs of another car, which might have brought the murderer, but the rain which had been falling was heavy enough to have obliterated any tyre marks.

Back in the house McLean showed Waller the two unidentified keys, and asked him if he knew what they fitted, but Waller denied all knowledge of them. In the dead man's bedroom there was nothing which needed a key, but in a drawer there McLean found a letter bearing no address, and written in a spidery hand. It said:

Must have a settlement within the next few days. You've been too long over this matter. I heard from W.W. that the stuff had gone through. So make it snappy. A.M.

'That could mean almost anything,' he mused. 'But persons who don't put their address on their note-paper, and use initials for their names usually have very good reasons for such omissions. Let's see what's upstairs.'

A secondary staircase led to three attic rooms. Two of these were open and empty, but the third was locked. McLean tried one of the spare keys and found it fitted. Inside was a collection of junk, and it seemed strange that Rossiter should want to lock up such rubbish. But McLean probed and finally found a black steel box under an old curtain.

'The last of our keys, I think,' he said.

In a few moments the box was open. On top were several old items of clothing, but underneath was as fine a collection of jewellery as McLean had ever seen. In a separate leather bag were many precious stones which had obviously been taken from settings, and that was significant enough to McLean.

'A burglar's hoard,' he said.

'And the murderer's objective.'

'I don't think so, for there's no evidence at all of any search here or elsewhere. I think we'll call it a day. But I want a word with Mr. Waller before we leave.'

They found Mr. Waller in the kitchen, drinking tea. McLean asked him the name of any solicitor whom Rossiter might have employed and was given the name of a firm in Ewell.

'Do you know any friend of Mr. Rossiter whose surname begins with an "M"?' McLean asked.

112

'Yes, sir. There's Mr. Markham. I don't know where he lives, but he's been here several times.'

'Alone?'

'No. Sometimes he came alone, and sometimes with another man. I think they were brothers. At any rate they looked very much alike.'

'Could they have been the two men you saw in a car when you left here this evening?'

'I wouldn't like to say that, sir. It was very dark and I saw almost nothing of their faces.'

'What about the car?'

'The last time they came they were driving a Ford. Am I to stay here the night, sir?'

'No. Have you anywhere else to go?'

'I've a married sister in Ewell.'

'I'll drop you there,' said McLean.

McLean did this on his way back to Scotland Yard. There he gave the candlestick to the fingerprints department, and then telephoned the dead man's son in Paris. Getting no response he asked the Paris police to get some information from him.

The next morning McLean heard that the candlestick was completely free from fingerprints, and a little later he was told by the French police that Rossiter's son had been in Paris all the previous day. He was employed by a reputable firm, and had an excellent character. He had been told of the death of his father and was at that moment on his way to London – by air.

While waiting for his arrival McLean had a talk with Rossiter's solicitor over the telephone. He knew nothing about the old man's source of income, except that he owned a number of houses in London. But Rossiter had made a will three years previously naming his son as his chief beneficiary, with a thousand pounds for Mr. Waller if he was still in Rossiter's service at his death.

'Nice little sum for Mr. Waller,' said Brook. 'His story of the two men in the car could have been an invention.'

'It could. But let us wait and see what the son has to say.'

An hour later the dead man's son arrived at Scotland Yard, and was taken at once to McLean's office. He was a man of about thirty-five years of age.

'It was good of you to come so quickly,' said McLean. 'When did you last see your father?'

'Three years ago. I came here for a short holiday.'

'What was he by profession, before he retired?'

'I don't think he ever had a profession. He had private means left him by his father. He was rather a curious man, and I'm sorry to say I never got on very well with him. We parted when I was only twenty. I was good at French and I found myself a job in Paris. We corresponded from time to time. But always he lived in a world of his own.'

'Did you ever meet a friend of his named Markham?'

'Yes. I was introduced to him when I stayed here. He was much younger than my father. A much travelled man. I think they met somewhere abroad. My father used to travel a lot in the past.'

'Did you meet Markham here?'

'No. We met at Markham's club, and had a meal with him.'

'What club?' asked McLean eagerly.

'Quite a small place, off Pall Mall. I think it was called the "Caxton".'

Brook gave McLean a quick glance, for the 'Caxton' was known to the police as a place with a sinister reputation. McLean thanked his informant and took the name of the hotel he proposed to stay at.

III

Immediately afterwards McLean visited the club, and found that Andrew Markham was still a member. His profession was given as engineer.

'Was he here last night?' asked McLean.

The steward reflected.

'Yes,' he said. 'I served him with a drink at about half-past seven. Then he went up to the card room and stayed there until about ten o'clock.'

'Was he alone?'

'No, he brought a guest with him. His brother I think.'

'Have you his private address?'

The steward went to the Secretary's office and came back with the address written on a piece of paper. A quarter of an hour later McLean was ringing the bell at

114

a flat in Shaftesbury Avenue. A thick-set dark man answered the summons.

'Are you Mr. Andrew Markham?' asked McLean.

'Yes. What can I do for you?'

'I wish to ask you some questions regarding a Mr. John Rossiter. I am a police officer.'

'Oh, please come inside.'

He led McLean and Brook to a well-furnished sitting-room, where another man, very like him, but a few years younger, was reading a newspaper.

'My brother, John,' he said. 'John, these gentlemen are police officers,' he explained.

'Indeed!' said John, and laid down the newspaper.

'When did you last see Mr. Rossiter?' asked McLean.

'It must be at least a month ago. Why do you ask? I hope nothing is wrong with him.'

'He was murdered last night!'

The two brothers expressed their horror very well.

'How ghastly!' said Andrew.

'What were your relations with Rossiter?' asked McLean.

'We were just friends. I met him in Nice about ten years ago and the friendship continued when we came back to England.'

'Were you engaged in any business together?'

'No.'

'Then can you explain this letter?' asked McLean, and handed him the letter which he had found in Rossiter's possession.

Markham stared at it and shook his head.

'This has nothing to do with me,' he said. 'The initials happen to be the same as mine, but I never wrote it.'

McLean walked across to a side-table on which rested a writing pad. He took out one of the sheets and held it up to the light. It had the same unusual watermark as the letter.

'The same note-paper,' he said.

'It is a very common brand.'

'What car do you run?'

'A Vauxhall.'

'Painted grey?'

'Yes.'

'Were you out in that car last night?'

'No.'

'What did you do from six o'clock onwards?'

'We were both here until about a quarter past seven. Then I suggested to my brother that he should come with me to my club and have a game of bridge. We arrived there on foot about half past seven, and stayed until ten o'clock. It is easily proved, if you need proof.'

'No,' said McLean. 'But I should like proof of your handwriting. Please write to my dictation on this sheet of paper.'

He read what was written on the letter which he had found, and Andrew wrote with his left hand. The result was nothing like the writing in the original letter. A little later McLean left them, but as he passed through the hall he saw the heads of two sets of golf clubs projecting from two bags, and his eyes gleamed.

'We're getting very warm, Brook,' he said, as they entered their car. 'Did you notice those golf clubs?'

'Yes, but why—?'

'Both lots were right-handed clubs. Most men who write with the left hand use left-handed clubs. But I've just remembered something else which may clear up an important matter. I want to see Mr. Waller again.'

Mr. Waller, when seen at his sister's house was most helpful.

'You have said that you lighted the two candles just before you left the house,' said McLean. 'Had the candles been used before?'

'No, sir. They were new ones which I took from a packet in the larder two days previously.'

'And it was at six o'clock when you lit them?'

'A minute or two afterwards.'

'Are there any fresh candles left in the packet?'

'Oh yes – about half a dozen.'

'Thank you.'

Brook did not get the gist of all this until McLean reached Scotland Yard, with the unused candles. He then proceeded to carry out an experiment. He lighted two of the new candles and then waited for them to burn down to the exact length of the two stumps which had been retrieved from the death-room.

'Twenty minutes only,' he said, as he looked at his watch. 'It means that Rossiter was struck down before half past six. The broken wrist-watch, with the hands at seven-twenty-six was a fake. The Markhams may have a good alibi for seven-twenty-six but they have none for six-twenty-six. Now for a search warrant.

That evening the search warrant was put into effect. McLean found nothing incriminating in the Markham's flat itself, but the personal search which followed yielded a thin piece of paper taken from Andrew's pocket. It was a receipt issued that day by a small dry-cleaning shop in Soho for one Harris tweed jacket. McLean got the jacket before the cleaner had started work on it. On the right sleeve was blood of an uncommon group, and it was significant that Mr. Rossiter's blood was of that same group. Both men were arrested and charged with murder. Andrew said nothing, but his brother, terrified by what faced him, was very vocal.

'It wasn't murder,' he said hysterically. 'He owed us money. We were all in the same game together, but Rossiter knew where to place the stuff. He was the cleverest fence in London. We went to his hide-out to frighten him into paying up. For a time it looked as if he would come clean. He went to the table to get the money and suddenly whipped out a pistol. My brother seized the candlestick and struck him first on the arm and then on the head. It was self-defence, not murder.'

Brook closed his shorthand note-book and McLean gave a little sigh of satisfaction.

12

OLD Mrs. Meadows sighed as she gazed from the channel steamer at the white cliffs of Dover which loomed out of the spring haze. Doreen West, her companion, who had been with her for many years, saw the joyful gleam in the old lady's eyes, and wrapped the rug closer round her.

'We're over half-way across,' she said. 'I dreaded we should have a rough crossing, but it's quite wonderful.'

'Yes, my dear – and how glad I am to be back again. If we only had a winter climate like the South of France no one would drag me away from England for four long months.'

'But you enjoyed it, didn't you?'

'At first. I always enjoy the change of food at first, but after a while I miss cook and her good English dishes. By the way you're sure you posted that letter to her, and to Mary?'

'Oh yes. I told cook to expect us about six o'clock, and to have dinner ready by seven.'

'But shall we really be home by six?'

'Upright says so. Having the car on the boat with us will save a lot of time. We should be on the road by half past two.'

Mrs. Meadows smiled and lay back and closed her eyes. She was over seventy years of age, but looked younger. Her comfortable circumstances were responsible for this. Every year she avoided the fogs and damp of England, and invariably came home when the English spring was breaking. For ten years she had been a widow – a very fortunate widow some said, inasmuch as her late husband had left her a fortune approaching a quarter of a million. The old house in Hampstead was now far too large for her, but she refused to sell it, and economized in staff by shutting off the whole of the top floor. It pleased her to hold this fort against the vast tide of new buildings, and but recently she had had the wall surrounding her lovely garden raised three feet to shut out the world.

'The daffodils can't be over yet,' she said. 'I hope Henry hasn't forgotten to dig out those new beds. He has such a shocking memory.'

'But he told you he had done so in his last letter,' said Miss West.

'Dear, dear – so he did. My memory isn't any better than his.'

Doreen West laughed, and then gave herself up to her book. Half an hour later the steamer docked. The car was got up from the hold, and Mr. Upright, the good-looking chauffeur performed miracles in getting it and the luggage through the customs.

'All ready, madam,' he said, finally.

'Splendid, Upright!'

The chauffeur closed the door behind the two ladies, and then seated himself before the wheel of the car. It moved away smoothly and Mrs. Meadows was indeed homeward bound. She slept most of the way, and was still asleep when the car passed through the gate of her property.

'Mrs. Meadows,' said Doreen, nudging the old lady's arm.

She woke up and stared through the window at the big cedar tree which drooped its long branches across the lawn near the house.

'Home!' she ejaculated. 'How nice! Oh, there's smoke coming from the chimneys. Yes, and I can see the new flower-beds. They look very nice. All I need now is a bath, a change, and a nice English dinner.'

'And then early to bed,' said Doreen.

Cook and the other maidservant welcomed their mistress in the hall, and the chauffeur disposed of the baggage. Doreen went upstairs to make sure the hot-water bottles were in the beds, and finally the home-coming was completed.

'Dead on time,' said Upright to Doreen. 'Didn't I tell you we should do it?'

'You were lucky,' replied Doreen. 'There was scarcely any traffic at all.'

'Only because I know the best way to dodge it. Well, I'm going to see what there is in the way of eats. Only sandwiches for lunch, and no tea. I could eat a horse.'

Doreen went to her own room, unpacked, and then took a bath in the second bathroom. When she had put on a clean frock she knocked on Mrs. Meadows's door, with a view to seeing if she could help her in any way. She got no reply, and wondered whether her employer had decided to take a nap. Opening the door softly she looked inside. There was no one in the bedroom, and several garments were lying across the bed. From the adjoining bathroom there came no sound. She went to the bathroom door, and listened. The dead silence continued. She rapped on the door.

'Mrs. Meadows!'

Alarmed by the absence of any response to a second louder call, she tried the handle of the door, but was unable to open it. She ran downstairs, and found Upright in the kitchen. He gazed at her frightened face.

'Anything wrong?'

'I – I don't know. Mary, did you prepare a bath for the mistress?'

'Yes, miss – as soon as she came in. I told her I had turned on the geyser and I think she went straight to the bathroom.'

'I can't make her hear – and the door is bolted on the inside. Upright – you must get that door open.'

.   .   .   .   .

McLean and Brook motored to the house in response to an urgent telephone message.

'Another bath tragedy,' said Brook. 'Remember the "Brides in the Bath" cases?'

'It's nothing like that,' said McLean. 'The victim is an elderly lady – a widow.'

They soon reached the house, and were let in by Miss West, who looked horrified and overwrought.

'The doctor is here,' she said. 'Mrs. Meadows's own doctor. This way please.'

They were taken to Mrs. Meadows's bedroom, where they found an elderly man busy with various instruments. He introduced himself as Doctor Coltman.

'What's the position?' asked McLean.

'She died ten minutes ago. Seven o'clock almost exactly.'

'Drowned?'

'I can't say. From the colour of the body I suspect carbon-monoxide poisoning, but her lungs were full of water. She was found completely immersed, but I understand she was raised above the water at once.'

'When did you receive the summons?'

'At six-forty-three. I came at once and arrived here at six-fifty-five. Since then I have been trying to revive her, but it was quite hopeless.'

'I understand you were her regular medical attendant?'

'Yes.'

'Had she heart trouble?'

'No. Her heart was as strong as might be expected for a woman of her age – seventy-two.'

'You are not prepared to give a certificate?'

'Not yet. A blood test is necessary. I would suggest the removal of the body.'

McLean was willing, and an ambulance was called. The coroner was communicated with, and then McLean proceeded to take evidence.

The companion – Miss West – gave her evidence in tears. She stated that she had been with Mrs. Meadows for just on ten years, and had been content in her post. She knew that Mrs. Meadows proposed having a bath before dinner, but she herself had not prepared the bath. Mary Lott, the maidservant, usually did that. It was only when she went to Mrs. Meadows's bedroom that she became alarmed.

'Who actually discovered the body?'

'I did. I got the chauffeur to break open the door, and immediately I saw Mrs. Meadows lying under the water. I cried out to the chauffeur to telephone the doctor, and then I raised Mrs. Meadows so that her head came above the water. She was a very short woman, and the bath was long for her.'

'What was the state of the bathroom when you entered?'

'It was foul. I noticed that the window was closed, and as soon as I had raised the body I opened the window.'

'Was the geyser alight?'

'Oh no.'

'I presume that is a private bathroom, reserved for Mrs. Meadows?'

'Yes. We have a second bathroom, on the next floor.'

'Has Mrs. Meadows ever complained about her bathroom?'

'Not to my knowledge.'

The next witness was Mary – a rather shy girl of about twenty years of age. She had been in the house just over a year, and had always prepared Mrs. Meadows's bath for her.

'She had one every morning at half past eight,' she said. 'I always brought her a cup of tea just before that time, and turned on the geyser for her, and brought her a fresh bath towel. I knew she'd want a bath this evening because she always does that after a long journey. It was about a quarter past six when I asked her if I should turn the water on, and she told me I might.'

'Did you then leave her?'

'Yes. The bath doesn't fill very quickly from that

geyser. I always used to leave her to turn it off when the bath was full enough.'

The chauffeur had little to say. He knew nothing about the bath until Miss West came rushing into the kitchen to ask him to force the bathroom door. She gave one look, and then told him to call the doctor, which he did at once.

'Mrs. Meadows had only just returned from abroad, hadn't she?'

'Yes. We've been staying at Mentone since November – Mrs. Meadows, myself and Miss West. We arrived at the house at six o'clock.'

'Was Mrs. Meadows all right during the journey by road?'

'I think so. She slept most of the way, but when we reached the house she woke up and seemed very pleased.'

'How long have you been chauffeur here?'

'Six years.'

'Did you always go away with her?'

'Yes. She liked having her own car wherever she was, and she was fussy about who drove her. I had to be careful to drive smoothly. She hated rapid acceleration, or rough braking. I got to know her ways.'

'Was the house closed during her absence abroad?'

'Yes. Only the gardener stayed on. He lives out, so didn't need to use the house.'

'When did the other servants return?'

'This morning, I think. Miss West wrote them to tell them we were returning today. She sent the key to the cook.'

The ambulance then arrived and the body was removed. McLean and Brook went to the bedroom, and from there passed into the bathroom. Originally it had been a dressing-room, and there was no communication with the corridor outside. The window was now open, and the water still in the bath. From the state of the water it was clear that Mrs. Meadows had started her ablutions before she was overcome. The gas geyser was on a shelf, with its pipe overhanging the bath. It was comparatively new, and of modern design.

'We'll try the geyser,' said McLean. 'Shut the door and the window.'

While Brook did this, McLean lighted the pilot jet

of the geyser and swung in the arm. The main jets came alight and very soon there flowed very hot water into the bath. McLean sat and waited, and in a few minutes he realized that something was wrong.

'The geyser's not functioning properly,' he said. 'The fumes are bad.'

'Can't smell 'em,' said Brook.

'You never had a nose worth using. The fumes are not getting away. They're coming out into the room. Poof! Open that window!'

'You're right,' said Brook. 'I suddenly got a whiff then.'

He flung open the window, and McLean turned off the geyser. He looked at the various joints, and then turned his attention to the flue-pipe. It went through the wall a little above the geyser, and came out on the other side to the left of the window. The fairly large cowl obscured the open end of the pipe, and the whole thing was too far away to be seen properly from the window.

'I think we'll get a ladder and have a look at it,' he said. 'If it appears to be in order we must get a gas-engineer here.'

They went downstairs and found a short ladder in a potting shed. Brook carried this to the spot where the flue-pipe came out of the wall. He went up it, and shone an electric torch under the cowl. McLean heard a low ejaculation.

'What did you say?' he asked.

'Blessed if it isn't a bird's nest – right inside the pipe. I'll have to bend the cowl back to get my hand down.'

'Don't!' called McLean. 'I'd like to see it.'

Brook descended the ladder, and McLean climbed up. Brook had already bent the cowl a little in order to see down the pipe, and now McLean saw the nest quite clearly. It was lying down close to the bend and was tight enough to prevent the functioning of the pipe. After a few moments he bent the cowl full over and managed to squeeze his hand inside the pipe and reach the nest. Slowly he came down the ladder.

'Is it a sparrow's nest?' asked Brook.

'I think so.'

'What a place to choose for rearing a family! Of

course the house has been shut up, and that accounts for it.'

'I'm not so sure,' said McLean. 'You can put the ladder away now.'

On entering the house McLean received a telephone call. It concerned the blood test which had been taken in the meantime.

'Carbon monoxide in the blood,' he said to Brook. 'Mrs. Meadows actually died from drowning, but she was first rendered unconscious by carbon monoxide. Whether that alone would have been fatal it is impossible to say. The fact is that being a short woman she slipped down in the bath and was drowned. So much for our bird's nest.'

'Then it's a straight case of misadventure?'

McLean shook his head slowly.

'It's murder,' he said. 'The bird's nest wasn't actually in the elbow of the flue-pipe. That's why I wanted to see it before you removed it. It was pushed down as far as a normal hand and arm would permit, but not far enough to give the impression of a natural nest. 1 admit that some birds do choose such places to build nests, but we have to bear in mind that a bird couldn't possibly have built a nest in that position. There must be some base – some foundation – for the nest. A bird isn't like a spider – it can't build mid-way between anything. I am convinced that this nest was taken from another place and deliberately pushed down the flue-pipe.'

'Phew!' whistled Brook. 'But aren't the circumstances just right?'

'Exactly right. The person who thought out the idea was intelligent. He might have gathered a nest which was quite out of keeping with its surroundings, but he didn't. He chose just the right kind of nest, and there was just room for a bird to get in under the cowl. But the nest was six inches above the elbow of the pipe. That gave the game away.'

'But who could have done it? It must have been in the pipe when Mrs. Meadows arrived home.'

'I think it was. We shall have to look into the financial side of the matter – find out who would benefit from Mrs. Meadows's death.'

There appeared to be no will in the house, so McLean found out the name of the dead woman's solicitor and got in touch with him at his house. Half an hour later the solicitor, much shocked, arrived at the house with Mrs. Meadows's will.

'My name is Twenn,' he said. 'Of Twenn & Twenn. I have acted for Mrs. Meadows for many years. This is her last will and testament, and it was executed three years ago.'

McLean read through the document. Despite the large amount of money involved it was a very simple will. Her beloved and trusted companion, Doreen West, was to receive the sum of £5,000. All other servants in her employ at the time of her death were to receive two years' wages. The residue was to be divided between her two nephews – John and Ralph Meeston.

'Do you know the nephews?' asked McLean.

'No. You will notice that both their addresses are Canadian. Their father had business interests there, and I think they went to Canada when they were quite young.'

Miss West was called, and on being questioned she stated that to the best of her knowledge the two nephews had not seen their aunt for five years, when they both came to London with their wives and families. Mrs. Meadows used to write to them about once a month. She had seen letters addressed to them.

Among some correspondence McLean found various letters from the Meestons. They were both in the same business in Toronto, and their letters were simple and affectionate. In one of them Ralph Meeston made a reference to his aunt's will. He said he thought she was being 'most generous' but hoped it would be many years before either he or his brother benefited financially by her good nature.

'It's necessary to know whether those two men were in Canada all the time their aunt was at Mentone,' said McLean. 'I'd better get through to Toronto.'

The call was put through, and later McLean had a talk with an official of the Canadian police. No reply could reasonably be expected until the following day, and the investigation was postponed until the following morning.

When the news from Canada came it was to the effect that both the Meestons had undoubtedly been at Toronto through the period when Mrs. Meadows was absent from her house. There was no evidence that any member of the Meeston family had left Canada.

'That seems to rule them out,' said Brook. 'The gardener has just arrived. Do you wish to see him now?'

McLean did, and the gardener was shown in. He was an elderly man of the retiring nervous sort. He was married and had four grown-up children. He said he had worked in the garden every day during Mrs. Meadows's absence, except Sundays and the Christmas holidays. He had never seen any callers, except a few 'touts', whom he turned away. He had been gardener there for over thirty years, and was quite obviously distressed at the thought of his early dismissal. When he had gone McLean shook his head.

'An honest, simple man I'm certain,' he said.

'Hear, hear!' commented Brook. 'With him ruled out, and the nephews, it leaves only Miss West and the chauffeur, who were both with Mrs. Meadows, and the cook and the pretty maid. It isn't likely that anyone would murder the old girl out of revenge. Mightn't the cook or the maid have a man friend who might guess they would come into some money in such an eventuality as this?'

'The cook is a widow and doesn't like men. I propose to question Mary, but I very much doubt if it will lead anywhere.'

When Mary was subsequently asked if she had a sweetheart she blushed and shook her head quickly. She added that she walked out with a boy over a year ago, but he began to 'drink awful' and in disgust she refused to see him again.

With no clue of any kind forthcoming from the evidence, or from the house, McLean went to the office and put in some work on the bird's nest, in company with a chemist. The nest was pulled to pieces bit by bit, and some interesting facts emerged. It was proved that the nest housed at least one brood of birds, for an egg had been broken in it, and the contents spread over some of the material of which it was made. It was now dried, but could not escape the skill of the chemist.

'A last year's nest,' said McLean. 'That bears out my contention that the nest was put there by human hands. What about that stain?'

A few minutes later the chemist was able to arrive at a decision.

'Black paint,' he said. 'A drip must have fallen from a brush into the nest. I have found traces of it on several bits of straw.'

'Thanks!' said McLean. 'That is interesting.'

Later in the day he went to the house. The gardener was at work, but the chauffeur had taken Miss West into town to do some shopping. When asked about black paint the gardener said he never did any painting. McLean went into the garage and looked into the interior of a cupboard. There he found cans of oil and paints of various colours. Among them was a tin of black paint, about half of which had been used. He called the gardener.

'Do you know what this pot was used for?' he asked.

'Why, yes – Mr. Upright painted the guttering of the garage last autumn. It was blocked up with pine needles, and he cleaned it out.'

McLean thanked him and inspected the guttering. The new paint was obvious. The guttering had been painted inside and out, and strangely enough at the junction of the drain-pipe there was a half-finished bird's nest, of exactly the same type as the one found in the flue-pipe.

'The lady sparrow is busy replacing her old nest,' he said to Brook.

'You mean that other nest came from here?'

'I think so. I know it was a last year's nest. Someone had allowed a drop of black paint to fall into it. Who could that person be but the man who painted the guttering? We had imagined that the nest was inserted in the flue-pipe during Mrs. Meadows's absence abroad, but that was wrong. I'm certain that it was put there after the bathroom was last used, and in readiness for Mrs. Meadows's return. That's a point I want to establish.'

Again the gardener was questioned. He said that it

was Upright's job to clean the windows. He did them every week, as part of his duties.

'Do you remember the day when Mrs. Meadows went abroad?' asked McLean.

'Yes, sir.'

'Did Mr. Upright happen to clean the windows that day?'

'Why, yes, he did, sir.'

'To do that he would use a ladder?'

'Oh yes. He did the outsides with a ladder. He did the windows during the morning. I remember seeing him.'

'Did you see him outside the bathroom?'

'No, I don't think I actually saw him there. But I think he did that window with the others.'

While they were talking Upright returned with Miss West, and McLean noted that Miss West was not sitting in the back of the car but next to the chauffeur. When she got out she seemed a little confused. He told her he wished to see her, and then conducted her into the house.

'Now, Miss West,' he said. 'I am going to ask you a very personal question, and I advise you to answer truthfully however embarrassing it may be.'

'I don't tell lies,' she replied sharply.

'Are you in love with Mr. Upright?'

She had certainly not expected this question, and her breast heaved.

'I – I can't see that that is of any interest—' she stammered.

'I must insist on a reply.'

'Well, yes I am.'

'How long has this been going on?'

'About six months—perhaps a little longer.'

'And he knows?'

'Yes. We are engaged.'

'Did Mrs. Meadows know?'

'No. I had intended to tell her when we arrived home, but there was no time.'

'I understand. Miss West, did Mrs. Meadows ever give you to understand that she would remember you in her will?'

The girl hesitated.

'Please answer.'

'Yes,' she said. 'Once she made a grim sort of jest. She had been ill, and was getting well again. She said to me, "Doreen, it was most unwise of you to nurse me back to health, because now you'll have to wait longer for your legacy." '

'You took that seriously?'

'I was rather hurt about it, and she knew it. She told me not to be so sensitive, and then said, "Would I have had a new will made and specially mentioned you if I didn't know how trustworthy you were." '

'You were bound to take that seriously?'

'Yes.'

'And did you ever tell anyone else?'

'My mother.'

'Anyone else?'

'I – I think I may have told Mr. Upright.'

'Before you went away to Mentone?'

'Yes – some time last summer.'

'That's all – thank you.'

McLean was now sure that he had all the facts. It would be a natural assumption that the bird's nest had been placed in the flue-pipe while the house was vacant – even if the police doubted its natural origin. Upright had a nice alibi for that period. What he didn't anticipate was the discovery of the evidence that an egg had been broken in the nest, and the spot of paint which marked him down as the culprit.

Before going farther the contents of the paint-pot were analysed. It proved to be of exactly the same ingredients as the spot of paint in the nest, and that on the guttering. The case now looked fairly good, but McLean wasn't sure it was good enough, and to make it so he indulged in a bold ruse. On the following day he arrested both Upright and Miss West. The former was charged with murder and Miss West with being an accessory.

'I thought you said she was innocent,' protested Brook.

'I did. But Upright is guilty and I believe he won't let the girl suffer unjustly. We'll see.'

His estimate of Upright's character was correct. Worn down by imprisonment – and perhaps by the conscious-

ness of his guilt – he called for McLean and made a
voluntary statement, which cleared Miss West completely.
After that he seemed much easier in his mind, although
he had, figuratively speaking, signed his own death warrant. McLean quoted Burns about there being 'good and
bad in the worst of us'.

13

PAUL LANCASTER and his wife had been hit rather
hard by the 'Credit Squeeze', for it had been put into
operation at the worst time so far as Lancaster was
concerned. It was customary for the bank to advance
him money periodically for the re-stocking of his small
business, but to his horror his latest application for this
temporary accommodation was politely but firmly turned
down.

'Here's a nice set-up!' he complained to his wife. 'The
stock is down to nothing. How can I keep going without
goods to sell?'

'Can't you get extra credit from the wholesalers?' asked
Mrs. Lancaster.

'Not enough. I've a pile of old accounts to settle. The
business is all right, but I must have a couple of thousand
quid – and quickly.'

Molly Lancaster thought for a moment.

'There's your Uncle Peter,' she ruminated. 'He's got
plenty of money, and you're his heir, aren't you?'

'So he says. But you know what he is. He wouldn't
lend me five hundred quid when I was in a bit of a
mess two years ago. It's all coming to me when he dies.
Wonderful how generous people can be when they are
dying.'

'Don't be cynical dear. I think he'd help if he knew
you were in a bad spot. He's about your only chance.
Why not invite him down here for the week-end? Give
him a good time, and then introduce the subject subtly.'

Lancaster frowned. He wasn't in love with his uncle,
whose tastes were quite different from his own, but
after thinking over his problem all night he fell in with

his wife's suggestion and drafted a pleasant letter to his rich relative.

'That ought to fetch him,' he said. 'I've mentioned that bit of rough shooting at Croxton, and told him to bring a gun. He loves shooting things.'

'You'd better lay in some whisky,' suggested Molly. 'I seem to remember he has a weakness that way.'

Uncle Peter accepted the invitation and the Lancasters did their best to give him a royal time with the object of softening him up. He came down to the country cottage in his big car, and was warmly welcomed and at once plied with a huge whisky and soda. The weather was wonderful and the view from his bedroom window was superb.

'That's the farm where I have some shooting rights,' said Lancaster, pointing to the distant farmhouse and its surrounding fields and woods. Plenty of wood-pigeons and quite a number of hares.'

The meal which followed was perfect. Molly had got out her best glasses, and whenever Uncle Peter's glass was getting low Lancaster replenished it. Molly, who hadn't had wine for a long time, was almost tipsy by the time the meal was over. Afterwards Lancaster and his uncle took their guns and came back at dusk with a couple of brace of wood pigeons. The old man was now in the sweetest of tempers.

Molly went to bed, leaving the two men talking together. Her husband joined her later. She gazed at him anxiously, but he shook his head.

'Too early to work on him yet,' he said. 'He asked about the business and I told him it was doing well. I just mentioned casually that the bank wasn't being very helpful, and he appeared to be sympathetic. But I dared not press the matter. Tomorrow I'll have a real go at him.'

The next day was as brilliant as the first. Uncle Peter was in good fettle.

'Don't worry about lunch, Molly,' he said. 'We'll go out somewhere in my car, and lunch will be on me. Ring up some place and book a table for three. Maybe we can take the guns out again in the evening, eh?'

'Of course,' said Lancaster.

Later they drove out in Uncle Peter's new Daimler,

131

and after visiting a number of beauty spots they finished up at a large and expensive hotel in most luxuriant grounds. Uncle Peter played the part of host most excellently, and quite a large number of pound notes changed hands when the bill was presented. In the evening, after Uncle Peter had had a nap, the shooting was most successful, for in addition to various birds Uncle Peter shot a large hare.

'There you are, Molly,' he said. 'He'll do for the pot, but you'd better hang him for a day or two. What a wonderful day it has been!'

'For us too,' said Lancaster. 'You must come more often, Uncle.'

'I will. By jove I will.'

Molly saw her husband in the passage as she was bringing in another bottle of whisky for the night-caps.

'Now's the time,' she whispered. 'You'll never get him in a better humour. I'll vamoose into the kitchen when I've had a drink. You lay into him then.'

'I will,' he promised.

But it all went wrong. When the two men were alone Lancaster mentioned the subject nearest his heart. He told his uncle of his predicament, and the old man listened attentively while he drank more of his nephew's whisky.

'Too bad!' he said when Lancaster had finished. 'How much are you needing to stock up the shop?'

'Two thousand pounds. It would only be for a short time, because—'

The telephone bell interrupted him, and he picked up the receiver.

'Yes,' he said, 'I'm Mr. Paul Lancaster. Oh, it must be my uncle you wish to speak to. One moment, please.'

'Someone wanting you uncle,' he said. 'Wouldn't give a name. I'll be back in a minute or two.'

He gave the old man the privacy of the room, and went into the kitchen where his wife was stacking up the dirty crockery.

'Well?' she asked.

'I had got him right up to the scratch when the darn telephone rang. Someone wanted to speak to him. I'll give him a few minutes and then tackle him again.'

But when he returned to the lounge Uncle Peter's mood had changed. He looked quite savage as he chewed a new cigar.

'My week-end ruined,' he growled. 'Bad news. I've got to pack and leave at once. Sorry about your little trouble. Wish I could help but I can't.'

II

It was ten o'clock the following morning when the Lancaster's were sitting in their garden reading the Sunday newspapers that they were surprised to see a police car draw up outside the gate, and from it stepped two men in plain clothes.

'Queer!' said Lancaster, and got up from his chair as the two men approached. The first was Inspector McLean and the second Sergeant Brook.

'Mr. Paul Lancaster?' asked McLean.

'Yes. This is my wife.'

'I am a police officer,' said McLean. 'Mr. Lancaster, did you write this letter?'

He produced an open envelope from his pocket and Lancaster recognized his own handwriting.

'Yes,' he said. 'It was to my uncle, inviting him to stay with us for the week-end.'

'Did he come?'

'Yes. He arrived on Friday evening, but left last night after receiving a telephone call. Is anything wrong?'

'I'm sorry to say there is. His dead body was found in his car early this morning near Esher.'

Lancaster gave a little gasp, and Molly stared as if she could not believe her ears.

'But he was quite well when he left here in his car,' she said. 'We both saw him off.'

'Did he have anything to drink before leaving here?' asked McLean.

'Plenty,' said Lancaster. 'He was rather fond of whisky, and had had rather a lot of it.'

'At what time did he leave?'

'It was about ten-twenty. We thought he was going to stay until Monday morning, but the telephone call caused him to change his mind, and he was in a dreadful hurry to get away.'

'Do you know who it was who telephoned?'

'No. It was a man who wouldn't give his name, but he seemed to know that my uncle was staying with us. I handed the receiver to my uncle, and left him alone.'

'At what time did that call come?'

'Round about ten o'clock. But please – please tell me what happened,' begged Lancaster.

'It is suspected that he died from poisoning, and there was nothing in the car to account for it.'

'But we shared the drink with him,' said Molly. 'Also the food which we had previously. There must be a mistake.'

'We shall know very soon. Some keys were found in his pocket, but nothing which gave his address. There has been no time yet to trace the car. Where did he live?'

'Number twenty flat, Carlton Mansions, Kensington,' said Lancaster.'

'Thank you,' said McLean. 'Did he live there alone?'

'Yes. He had a woman who looked after him, but only on a daily basis.'

'Can you tell me something about him?'

'Not a lot. He was my father's only brother. I think he was left a good deal of money by my grandfather. He liked travel, and for many years was abroad. He never married so far as I know.'

'Did he follow no profession?'

'No. He seemed to be able to live quite well on his inheritance. Since my father's death eight years ago I have only seen him about half a dozen times. I think his age would be about sixty – two years older than my father.'

McLean then told him that he would be needed to identify the dead man, but the next day would do. Then he and Brook went back to the car and drove towards London.

'Are they all right?' asked Brook.

'Who can say at this juncture? Drive to Carlton Mansions and we'll see what we can learn there.'

One of the dead man's keys fitted the door of the flat, and very soon McLean was probing into everything. He found a great number of vouchers for interest on Government Bonds, and various share certificates for large amounts, also a bank statement showing £18,000 on deposit.

'Evidently a man of wealth,' he said. 'Altogether these things represent a capital of over £40,000. Ah, what's this?'

It was a strong blue foolscap envelope marked 'Peter Lancaster Esquire – PRIVATE,' and the contents was a will, dated seven years earlier. McLean read it carefully.

'Very brief,' he said. 'He leaves everything to his nephew, Paul Lancaster.'

Brook gave a low whistle.

'That smells a bit,' he said.

Then the telephone bell rang, and McLean went to the instrument and picked up the receiver.

'Miss Dickenson?' he said. 'No, I am not Mr. Lancaster. Wait a moment. I will inquire.'

He placed his hand over the mouthpiece.

'A young woman – rather excited,' he said. 'Wants to speak to the dead man. I can't miss this opportunity.'

He waited a little longer and then spoke again.

'Mr. Lancaster is not available now,' he said to the caller. 'But could you possibly call here fairly soon?'

'Yes. Tell him I'll be there in a quarter of an hour.'

McLean was still going through documents when the doorbell rang.

'That must be Miss Dickenson,' he said. 'Go and let her in, Brook.'

Brook came back with a good-looking woman of about thirty years of age. She was dressed rather flashily, and stared at McLean as she entered the room.

'I – I thought—' she stammered.

'I am Inspector McLean of Scotland Yard,' said McLean. 'I am here investigating the death of your friend Mr. Peter Lancaster. Please sit down.'

Miss Dickenson collapsed in the chair rather than sat. Her lower lip trembled and tears came to her eyes.

'What – what happened?' she stammered.

'He was found dead in his car early this morning. Is your Christian name Monica?'

'Yes.'

McLean extracted from some documents a bank statement for the dead man's current account. He ran a finger down the list of debits.

'Here it is,' he said. 'Miss Monica Dickenson – £2,000. Paid on June the first. Can you explain that payment?'

'Yes. I wanted to start a little business and he put up the money.'

'What sort of business?'

'A club. It's called "The Sunflower", and is in Great Portland Street.'

'Is there any sort of business contract?'

'No. I was to pay him back – when I could.'

'Did you not know that Lancaster was spending the week-end with his nephew?'

'No. He never told me.'

'Do you know anyone who had cause to hate him?'

'No.'

'When did you last see him?'

'On Thursday night. He came to the club and played bridge with some members.'

When she had gone McLean stroked his jaw reflectively.

'Curious sort of man,' he said, to lend a woman two thousand pounds, without security of any sort. I don't think she's a very reliable witness.

Later in the day McLean heard that poison had been found in Lancaster's organs, and that death had been due to that. The medical opinion was that he would have died within an hour of having taken it.

'The question is, where did he get the poison? It could have been at his nephew's house, or at some other place at which he called. Our next job is to have a look at his car.'

III

Later the big Daimler was examined with great care. It was scrupulously clean with the exception of the rubber-covered accelerator pedal, on which was a coating of sticky grey mud. This puzzled McLean, for there was no mud at all on the dead man's shoes. He saw the officer who had driven the car to police headquarters and asked him about the mud.

'It was there when I took over the car, sir,' he said.

'Thank you. I thought it was.'

'So Lancaster didn't drive the car to the spot where it was found?' said Brook.

'No. He stopped somewhere and had a drink. It certainly wasn't a pub, because no pub would have been open at that time in that area. The presumption is he went to a house, and was poisoned there. Later his body was put in the car and driven away from the place. It was somewhere between his nephew's cottage and Esher, I imagine.'

'Then it must have been somebody he knew and trusted?'

'Yes. It all links up with that telephone call. Someone gave him a message which caused him to pack up at once, and, I think, call on that person. We might do worse than have a look at the Sunflower Club.'

They visited the place later in the evening. It comprised four rooms on the ground floor, one of which was the bar. About a dozen men and women were present, drinking heavily. The man behind the counter said that Miss Dickenson was in the office along the passage, so McLean and Brook went and knocked on the door. Miss Dickenson let them in.

'I should like to see the list of club members,' said McLean.

Miss Dickenson produced the book. There were some fifty names in it, most of them with London addresses. Among them was Peter Lancaster. Among the country members was the name Henry Gissing, of Hook, and McLean remembered that Hook was two miles west of Esher.

'You have said that last Thursday Lancaster was here playing bridge with other members. Can you remember who they were?'

'Yes. One was Mr. Edwards, of Chelsea. There was one woman – Miss Akers. The fourth was Mr. Gissing.'

'Is he in the club now?'

'No.'

'Nor Mr. Edwards?'

'Yes, he's here.'

'Will you ask him to come here?'

Miss Dickenson went out and soon returned with an old roué who was a little the worse for drink. But he remembered the bridge party.

'Did you hear Mr. Lancaster say that he was spending the week-end with his nephew?' asked McLean.

'That's right,' he hiccuped. 'Said he was going to see him the next day.'

'Was Mr. Gissing present then?'

'Yes.'

'Were he and Lancaster good friends?'

'Like brothers. They were in business together years ago. Made a lot of money – some foreign place. China I think.'

'Does Gissing come here often?'

'Not often. He's a mighty sick man. Going to have a major operation soon.'

McLean thanked him, and let him go. Then he turned to Miss Dickenson, who was looking far from happy.

'Your friend Lancaster was murdered,' he said. 'You still haven't explained that loan of two thousand pounds to my satisfaction. What were your real relations with Lancaster?'

'He – he was my lover,' she said. 'Until a few months ago. We were to be married, but for some reason he backed out. He gave me the money to prevent a breach of promise action. I swear I know nothing about his death.'

'What do you know about his association with Gissing?'

She hesitated for a moment.

'I don't think Gissing really liked him,' she said. 'I know that Gissing used to borrow money from him, and pretended he was his bosom friend, but somehow I had the feeling that Gissing was concealing something.'

It was dusk that evening when McLean and Brook stopped their car outside a bungalow at Hook. There was a light in one of the bedrooms, but the lower part of the place was in darkness. Just inside the garden gate was a half-dried patch of grey mud, and on it some footprints. There were also signs of footprints avoiding the muddy portion.

'One man went round, the other wasn't so careful,' said McLean.

A ring at the door bell brought no response. McLean tried again with no better result. Then he tried the handle and found that the door was not locked. He went inside and called up the stairs loudly. No answer came back.

138

'I'm going up, Brook,' he said.

In the lighted bedroom an ashen-faced man lay across the bed. McLean picked up one of the hands. It was stone cold. On the table was a small blue bottle placed on a letter. The bottle was marked 'Poison' and was empty. McLean picked up the letter and read some pencilled scrawl across the top of it.

'Can't face the operation. Better this way, now I've wiped off an old debt. Telephoned him to say I was dying, and the fool took the bait. Letter will explain.
Robert Gissing.'

The letter did explain. It was from a man in Hong-Kong dated two months back. It said:

Have discovered beyond doubt that the man who gave you away, and sent you to jail for seven years was your old pal Pete Lancaster. Inspector Roberts died here two days ago. He told me with his dying breath. What are you going to do about it?

'I think we know exactly what he did,' said McLean. 'Well, it will save quite a lot of trouble.'

14

ON a few rare occasions Inspector McLean ran into crime, instead of having it served up to him. So used was he to the latter process that he resented these busman's holidays, which seemed to him to be a quite unwarrantable departure from the orthodox. Such a thing happened to him on his way north to attend a conference connected with his calling.

It was to be a four-hour train journey, but this promised to be no great ordeal, since he had scarcely had a moment to call his own for the past month. Browsing over the bookstall he had selected three magazines containing rather weighty matter, and these, he thought, would occupy his mind for the whole journey. It was a lovely spring afternoon, and the compartment which he chose on the train was in a brand new coach and as clean and comfortable as he had ever experienced.

Few people were travelling on that train, and up to a few minutes before it was due to steam out of the London terminus it looked as if he would have the whole carriage to himself. This, with the first stopping place two hours distant, was pleasant to contemplate.

But at the last moment his hope was blighted, for into the compartment came a girl, followed by a porter carrying a hat-box and a large suitcase. She passed McLean, who was sitting next to the corridor, and bagged the seat in the corner on the farther side of the compartment. The porter put her belongings into the rack above her head.

'Just in time, Miss,' he said. 'There goes the whistle.'

She fumbled in her handbag and produced a shilling, which she gave to the cheerful porter.

'Thank you, Miss,' he said. 'Pleasant journey. Lord, they're quick off the mark.'

The next moment he was leaping along the corridor, and McLean saw him drop neatly to the platform as the train was moving. After that there was silence, and McLean worked his way through what was intended to be a searching analysis of the Nazi mind. The writer of the article was setting out to prove that Hitler had been the victim of a form of sexual repression, when McLean noticed that his travelling companion was weeping quite copiously into a diminutive handkerchief. He gave an inward sigh, for nothing was so disturbing to his peace of mind as a weeping woman.

He raised his eyes above the printed page, and saw her clearly for the first time. She appeared to be about twenty years of age, well dressed, and fair of complexion. Her hands were small and shapely, and her finger-nails were the colour nature intended them to be. Weeping had reddened her exquisite little nose, and altogether detracted from her good looks. The regular sniffing ruined the picture altogether.

Suddenly she raised her eyes, and realized that she was being observed. Giving a final sniff, she crumpled up the handkerchief and rammed it into her handbag. Then shook her head in a kind of resolute manner.

'Sorry,' she murmured.

'Not at all,' responded McLean. 'But it's scarcely the sort of day for lamentation.'

'No. It was silly of me. I won't do it again.'

McLean smiled and got his attention back on the magazine. For the best part of an hour he read solidly, and then the restaurant man barged in with the information that tea was now being served. McLean shook his head, but the girl put a bit of powder on her nose, and then left the compartment.

McLean's second literary course was a brilliant description of the life cycle of the Liver Fluke. It was rather more to his taste than probing the dark mind of dead 'overlords' of Europe, and he spent quite a long time on it. Finally he closed the magazine, and let his gaze reach out to the sunlit meadows through which the train was passing. Then it occurred to him that his late travelling companion was spending an inordinately long time over tea – especially the sort of tea one got on trains. But perhaps she was attempting to restore her lost beauty.

'Tickets, please!' chanted the ticket-collector as he slipped through the sliding-door.

McLean yielded up his ticket for punching, and then the official turned his gaze to the girl's baggage.

'Having tea,' explained McLean.

When the official had gone McLean lapsed into a reverie which was very near to sleep. He was brought to full consciousness by the obvious application of brakes, and the train slowed down and finally came to a standstill beside a platform. McLean got up and strolled into the corridor. Through an open window he was able to see the tall spire of the ancient and beautiful cathedral, and while he admired that poem in stone he became aware that the restaurant-car was being taken off. This was no loss to him, as the train was due at his destination in time for him to have a meal before attending the conference.

The train soon moved on again, and he still reigned in solitary state. But what of his travelling companion? Had she found a friend in another compartment, or was she still engaged in removing the blemishes of her recent breakdown?

A long time passed and still she failed to appear. McLean gave up thinking about the matter, and occupied himself with another magazine. In due course he reached his destination, which was also the terminus of that particular train, and still the hatbox and the suit-case rested on the rack. Neither of them bore a label, but the suitcase had the initials N.G.N. stamped on it in black letters. McLean waited a minute or two, and while he did so the ticket-collector came along.

'As far as we go, sir,' he said.

'I know that. I'm wondering what happened to my travelling companion whom I haven't seen for the past two hours. That's her luggage.'

'Hm!' said the ticket collector. 'That's funny. Every-one is off the train. But I'll make sure.'

He was absent for some minutes, and finally he came back alone.

'No one left,' he said. 'Well, they'll have to go to the "left luggage" department. Funny how absent-minded some people are. You'd be surprised at the things that are left in railway trains. Why, I've known a woman leave her baby behind.'

'That mightn't have been absent mindedness,' said McLean.

The ticket collector took the two articles from the rack, and fingered the catches.

'Both locked,' he said. 'Well, there's nothing we can do about it but wait until they're claimed. What sort of a person was she?'

McLean described the girl briefly, and then, having wasted enough time on a matter which he felt was none of his business he went on his way.

The conference proved to be a most boring affair. Many persons spoke who would have done better to have remained silent. The whole thing added nothing to McLean's knowledge of anything, and when finally he got back to his hotel he was of the opinion that he had wasted his time, and the country's money.

He planned to catch an early train back to London the following morning, and would have done so but for one thing. That thing was an item of dramatic news in the morning newspaper. It stated that a young woman had been picked up on the permanent way of the Southern Railway the preceding afternoon. Her name, as given on some cards in a handbag found near her, was Norah Nelson. She was suffering from serious injuries, and was unconscious. It was feared she would not survive her injuries, nor be able to explain how the accident occurred.

II

The train which McLean had proposed catching was a non-stop express, and McLean's new intention rendered it useless to him. There was no doubt in his mind that the injured girl was his late travelling companion, and he could not easily accept 'accident' as the cause of her tragic adventure. Suicide it might be, but that too he doubted.

Remembering the left luggage he decided to pay a visit to the lost property office, before catching the slow train which was scheduled to stop at the town where the injured girl had been taken, since it was possible that the clerk in charge of the office might not connect the lost luggage with the victim of the tragedy.

This indeed was the case. The man in question was very old and far from bright. It took quite a long time for him to understand exactly what McLean was driving at, and then it took him almost as long to turn up the details in his book. At last he found the items.

'Ah,' he said. 'Here they are – hatbox and brown leather suitcase bearing initials N.G.N. Taken off three-twenty-five train from London by ticket collector, J. Emerson. Claimed last night by a Miss Nelson, looks like Nelson to me.'

He pointed out the bad signature to McLean, who gave a little hiss of surprise.

'Did you attend to the lady?' he asked.

'Come to think of it – I did. Must have been round about eight o'clock. She said she had left two articles in the train, and she described them to my satisfaction.'

'Didn't you ask her to open the suitcase?' asked McLean.

'No. She gave all the required details.'

'What was she like?'

The old man regarded McLean searchingly. He was clearly getting fed up with this cross examination.

'Are you interested in the young lady?' he asked.

'I am, and so will you be when I tell you that there is good reason to believe that the real owner of those articles fell from the train yesterday a hundred miles down the line.'

The old man's protruding windpipe moved up and down in his uncontrollable perturbation.

'You mean she – the young woman who called here – wasn't the person she pretended to be?' he gasped.

'I do. What was she like? Come, I'm a police officer. What was the woman like?'

This question was beyond the power of the old man to answer with any satisfaction. The light was bad, he explained. He knew she was young, but he hadn't taken much notice of her. Finally McLean considered he was wasting his time, so he went in search of his train.

Some three hours later he stood by a bed in a hospital on the fringe of a small country town, looking down at the heavily bandaged form of a young woman. Beside him was an official of the County Police whom he had seen in the meantime.

'It's the woman I travelled with,' said McLean. 'There's no doubt at all about that.'

'Then the other woman was an impersonator?'

'Yes. That fact suggests foul play. The natural deduction is that Miss Nelson was deliberately pushed from the train while it was in motion, and that her attacker continued on his journey to the terminus. He probably wanted to take the suitcase, and the hatbox, but saw me in the compartment. When the articles were removed by the railway official and taken to the lost luggage department, he employed the woman to gain possession of them. Unfortunately he was successful.'

He turned to the house surgeon who had accompanied them and questioned him upon the chances of the girl's recovery. This gentleman was not very hopeful.

'She had a blood transfusion early this morning,' he said. 'So far she hasn't reacted. Of course there may be a change, but I have grave doubts.'

'Has she said anything at all since she has been here?'

'Not a word.'

McLean went back to police headquarters, where he was shown the handbag which had been picked up on the railway track. It contained some printed cards, giving the girl's name, but with no address. The other articles were a compact, a cigarette case and a book of strip matches, three keys, and six pounds odd in cash. There was no railway ticket, and McLean concluded that this had been collected. He shook the apparently empty handbag over a table, and something fell from it and rolled to the floor. It was only a scrap of paper, twisted into a spiral. McLean untwisted it, and found it to be a telegram dated the previous day, and addressed to 'Nelson, 12a Tresham Mansions, N.W.' The text was brief. It said:

Get package from safe deposit. Bring it on earliest train. Don't worry. Pop.

'Handed in at Baxmouth,' said McLean. 'From where I've just come, and to which place the girl was apparently going. The trouble is we don't know exactly where she was going in Baxmouth. But there may be a clue at the London address. Will you leave this in my hands at the moment?'

'Certainly. We shall be glad of your help.'

McLean continued his journey to London, and very soon after his arrival there he went to the address contained in the telegram, taking with him Sergeant Brook whom he quickly put in possession of the salient facts.

'I imagine one of these keys is her door key,' he said. 'As I haven't had time to get a search warrant, I hope it is.'

Number 12a Tresham Mansions was hidden away in a vast pile of brick and mortar, which had sprung up since McLean was last in the district. After walking several lengthy corridors McLean found the flat. He made a guess at the door key, and was right in his guess. A few moments later they were inside a very modern self-contained apartment.

'What I want is the address of the sender of the telegram,' said McLean. 'It may be here.'

'Won't the post office have it – on the original telegram?'

'Yes. The country constabulary looked into that while I was on my way back. The address written by the sender of the telegram has no existence.'

'All very sinister,' said Brook. 'Here's a key, stamped Union Deposit Company.'

McLean took the key, and examined it.

'This bears out the telegram,' he said. 'She evidently collected the parcel and was on her way to "Pop", whom I presume is her father. The object of the interception seems clear enough. The immediate need is to locate the father.'

A number of letters were found, but none of them seemed to have any connexion with Baxmouth. McLean retained them with a view to getting further evidence from the writers. Then, in a short feminine coat a letter was found bearing the address of a Baxmouth nursing home. It made the position clear. The man, who signed himself 'Pop', was waiting to undergo an operation. Evidently the girl had previously asked if she should go to Baxmouth to be near him, but he said it wasn't necessary. He was quite sure everything would be all right, and she wasn't to worry about him.

'Written three days ago,' said McLean. 'Get me the nursing home on the telephone. Here's the number.'

The number was connected after some delay, and McLean asked after a patient named Nelson. He was informed that a Thomas Nelson died during the night after undergoing a serious operation. The nursing home had been trying to ring up his daughter, but had been unable to get in touch with her. McLean spoke for a few minutes and then hung up the receiver.

'The solution lies at Baxmouth,' he said. 'Nelson was taken ill at the house of a friend, while visiting Baxmouth. He was removed at once to the nursing home, but the operation he needed had to be postponed in view of his poor general state of health. But let's see how the girl is faring.'

His inquiry at the hospital where Norah Nelson lay produced the reply that she was still unconscious, and still in great danger. It threw McLean back on the friend at Baxmouth with whom Nelson had stayed so recently.

'The girl may die,' he said. 'Then it will be murder. I think Baxmouth is clearly indicated. Look up a train.'

So again McLean did the lengthy railway journey, taking Brook with him. An examination of the dead man's effects shed no light on the matter, and he finally went to the address which the Matron gave him. It was a large house far away from the centre of the town, surrounded by an old-world garden which appeared to be much overgrown. On ringing the bell the door was opened by an elderly manservant who limped badly. McLean asked if Mr. Valli was at home, and the manservant said he would find out.

'What name, please?' he asked.

'Inspector McLean.'

A minute or two later McLean and Brook were shown into a large untidy room where a middle-aged man was sitting by a fire. He was swarthy and looked Italian or Spanish. McLean apologized for the late call, and explained partially the object of his visit.

'Oh, Nelson,' said Valli. 'I heard the bad news earlier in the evening. I had no idea the operation would be such a serious one. When he called on me I thought he looked ill. He collapsed in this room, and I had to call a doctor.'

'I know that,' replied McLean. 'What I wish to know are facts about Mr. Nelson. How long have you known him?'

'Many years. I knew him in Barcelona before the terrible civil war. He and I both managed to get away in time. He was a widower with a young daughter at school here. She used to come to Spain at intervals.'

'What was Mr. Nelson doing in Spain?'

'He was in a shipping office. I was an exporter of oranges, so our friendship had a business basis.'

'When was he last here?'

'Six days ago. He came down about a post in Baxmouth, and he spent the night here. It was on the following morning that he came over ill, and was taken to the nursing home.'

'Did you write to his daughter?'

'No. I was going to wire her, but he begged me not to. He said he would write, and make light of his pending operation, because she was the sort of girl who would worry unduly.'

'Did you know that he finally telegraphed for her to come down here?'

'No. When was that?'

'Shortly before he was due to have his operation.'

'That's curious. I got the impression that he didn't want her close at hand. Did she come?'

'She started, but she never got here,' replied McLean.

'I don't understand. Was she taken ill on the way or something?'

'She was pushed out of a train, and found later suffering from injuries which may yet prove fatal. Unfortunately she has been unconscious ever since she was picked up, and so we have no means of knowing exactly what took place.'

'Great Heavens! How shocking. But why was she attacked like that?'

'This is what I want to find out. Can you help me in any way?'

'I wish I could, but I haven't an idea in my mind. When I last saw the girl she was only a stripling. That was years ago. I know that Nelson was devoted to her. He had hoped to send her to a University, but the civil war came, and put an end to his business. He got away by the skin of his teeth.'

'When did you last see Nelson?'

'On Tuesday afternoon at the nursing home. He told me he was going to be operated on very shortly—'

He was interrupted by the intrusion of a young woman, who hesitated, and apologized as she saw that Valli had visitors.

'It's all right, Inez,' he said. 'Just a matter of business. Did you want me?'

'I only wanted to say good night,' she lisped.

'Good night, my dear.'

'My daughter,' said Valli, when she had gone. 'I thought it best not to tell her about that poor girl. She's been through enough trouble already.'

'Do you and she live alone here?' asked McLean.

'Yes. The house is miles too big, but I got it cheap. She yearns to go back to Spain, but I am not popular with the present Spanish government, so that's impossible – yet.'

'So you can't help me?'

'No, I regret to say. I wish you would let me know where the girl is. I should like to see her when she is able to receive visitors. Her father would have wished that.'

'I'll let you know,' promised McLean.

McLean was reflective when he and Brook got back into the car. For reasons of his own he had not told Valli that he knew the call to Norah Nelson had not come from her father. Nelson, had he sent the telegram, could only have done so through the nursing home, and its origin would then have been truthfully included. He began to theorize audibly.

'Someone interested in the package which Nelson kept in a safe deposit, knew that Nelson was soon to undergo a very serious operation,' he said. 'Look at the situation from that person's point of view. If Nelson died the package would be brought to light, and dealt with by the liquidator of Nelson's estate. Our unknown man's chances of getting hold of it would be nil. So the telegram to the girl was quite a good idea. Now few people could have known that Nelson was in any danger of losing his life. One of them was undoubtedly Mr. Valli, and he happens to have a daughter, who could have collected those articles that were left in the train, but our trouble is that the old man in the lost property office wouldn't know her from Eve. Of that I am convinced.'

'But she signed for the articles,' said Brook, brightly.

'Yes – in very bad light, with a pencil. To get a specimen of her normal handwriting may not be easy. Still we must try.'

'There's just one point concerning Valli,' said Brook. 'He stated that he was with Nelson on Tuesday afternoon. That was the day the girl travelled down here. If that's the truth he's got a perfect alibi.'

'I realized that,' said McLean. 'That is why we are now going to the nursing home.'

At the nursing home it was very quickly established that Valli's statement was true. He had been in the nursing home at the moment when Norah Nelson was on the west-bound train. By no means could he have boarded the train.

'That eliminates him,' said Brook.

Again McLean telephoned the hospital where the injured girl lay, and again he was told the same thing. No change.

'There's nothing more we can do until tomorrow,' he

said, 'I want the signature for the two articles of lost luggage, and also the original telegram.'

Early the following morning the investigation was resumed. McLean went to the lost property office first, and found again the old dotard in charge. He asked to see the signature of 'Norah Nelson' and the old man produced the book. But on turning to the requisite page a new development came to light. The faked signature of 'Norah Nelson' had been completely obliterated by a particularly heavy pencil. Not a trace of it was left.

'Well!' gasped the old man.

'Never mind,' said McLean, a little bitterly.

'Someone works fast and well,' muttered Brook, as they went back to the car.

'Yes. It was no use going into "hows" and "wherefores". It wouldn't get us anywhere. Let's try the G.P.O.'

Here there was no hold-up. The official whom McLean saw was very alert and helpful, and in a short time the original telegram was lying on his desk. But to McLean's disappointment it was written entirely in very conventional block letters.

'Stumped again,' growled Brook.

McLean turned the telegram form over. The spurious address was also in block letters. For a moment it seemed useless, and then McLean's sensitive nose came to his assistance. He brought the telegram closer to this well-developed organ, and sniffed.

'There are times when I curse my fantastic sense of smell,' he said. 'But there are also times when it is useful. What do you make of that, Brook?'

Brook smelt the telegram.

'Nothing,' he said.

'Well I do. It's scented, and my guess is Molyneux Numero Cinq.'

'Numero what?'

'Very popular, my dear Brook. Go to any place frequented by the fair sex and the atmosphere reeks with it. Yes – Molyneux Numero Cinq.'

'The lady again?' asked Brook.

'I think so. You'll observe that the telegram has been folded twice. If it was written in a post office there would be no need to fold it. I surmise it was written in a house, and folded to get it into a handbag. In short, I believe it was written by Valli, and taken to the post office by his charming daughter.'

'But Valli has an alibi—'

'Quite possibly, but I'm still interested in Miss Valli's handbag. This would be a good time to catch her at home.'

When they reached the house McLean was informed that Mr. Valli and Miss Valli were at breakfast, but he was insistent, and was finally shown into the dining-room.

'I'm sorry to intrude like this,' he said. 'But I wanted to show you this telegram. Did you write it, Mr. Valli?'

'Good gracious, no,' replied Valli, as he scanned the telegram.

'Then perhaps Miss Valli wrote it?'

The girl shook her head, as she gave the telegram a casual glance.

'I do not know Miss Nelson,' she said. 'But I have heard her father speak of her.'

McLean's roving gaze had already spotted a handbag, lying on the sideboard.

'Is that yours, Miss Valli?' he asked.

'Yes,' she replied.

'I should like to look inside it.'

He did not wait for her consent, but snapped the thing open. The first thing he came upon was a nice lace handkerchief. It was obviously a clean one, but both it and the handbag reeked with scent.

'So you took the telegram even though you may not have written it,' he said to her.

Valli stood up before the girl could reply.

'Really, Inspector, this is intolerable—'

'Mr. Valli,' cut in McLean. 'Please don't interrupt. This may be a case of murder. Push that bell behind you.'

Valli gulped, and pushed the bell automatically. A few moments passed, and then the sinister manservant entered.

'What is your name?' asked McLean.

'Gonzales, sir.'

'You will stay here with Mr. and Miss Valli. I propose to search the house.'

'You have no right—' protested Valli.

'Look after them, Brook,' said McLean.

For a long time the search looked like being a failure. There was not a sign of either the hatbox or the suitcase which McLean had seen in the train, nor was there anything else of an incriminating character. McLean realized that he had nothing really substantial against the trio, especially against Valli, who had a perfect alibi. He was about to give up when he noticed a small amount of soot in the library fireplace. This was all the more significant as the fireplace now housed a large electric fire. He removed this and investigated the wide chimney. There was a recess about two feet up, and in this was a flat box. He drew it out, and found it to be a large jewel case. The lock had been forced, and on opening the lid he came upon a marvellous collection of jewels. When he brought this into the sitting-room the three prisoners looked very sick. But Valli soon recovered his wits.

'My family jewels,' he said.

'You will need to explain the crest on the outside,' snapped McLean. 'You are all under arrest.'

.   .   .   .   .

Twenty-four hours later Norah Nelson won her battle, and came to full consciousness. She was still too ill to be questioned, but she was able to identify the man who had met her in the corridor of the train, and pushed her out on the line. It was Gonzales. She didn't know why, since he was a stranger to her, nor did she know what the parcel had contained.

'Her father never confided in her,' McLean explained to Brook. 'But Gonzales, having missed the hangman's noose has made it clear. The owner of the jewels is a Spanish nobleman, who is still languishing in a Spanish jail. Old Nelson was his friend and confidante. He smuggled the jewels into England, and was keeping them against the release of his friend. Valli, while pretending to be Nelson's friend, was all the time planning to get those jewels back into Spain. When he believed that Nelson might die he took a desperate step. It very nearly came off.'

'Funny how you came to catch that particular train.'

'Not so funny,' retorted McLean. 'I don't like these busman's holidays.'

15

ARNOLD BENTLEY, the senior partner in the firm of
Bentley Brothers, stormed into the office where his
brother was checking some accounts. 'That girl will have to go,' he said. 'It's half past nine
and she hasn't put in an appearance. This happens about
three times a week.'
His brother James initialled an item and looked up
at him.
'Laura?' he asked.
'Who else would it be. She's no good Jim. Ever since
she won that beauty competition last summer her head
has been up in the clouds. Her mind isn't on the job,
and she's rude to some of our best customers.'
James looked worried rather than annoyed. He had
been on the friendliest terms with Laura Lessing's
parents before they had been killed in a dreadful car
accident, and felt a sense of responsibility for the highly-
strung impulsive daughter.
'She's very young, Arnold,' he said. 'I think a little
straight talk will bring her to her senses.'
'I've already tried that,' said his brother.
'Well, let me have a go as soon as she arrives.'
'All right, but I wish I could feel it would do any
good. She's quite out of hand.'
It was ten minutes later that there was a knock on the
office door, and Laura entered. She was certainly an
attractive creature, with her mass of fair hair, and limpid
blue eyes. She was modestly dressed, for the firm would
not tolerate any plunging necklines or exposed calves.
But there was a haughtiness in the way she held her
head, and an obvious consciousness of her physical pro-
portions.
'I'm sorry I'm late, Mr. Bentley,' she said.
'I'm sorry too, Laura. This is not the first time you
know.'
'It's the bus that's the trouble. If I miss the eight-
thirty I have to wait a full half hour.'
'I know. But why miss the bus so often?'
'I had a very late night. Went to a dance.'

'But your lateness is not all, Laura. My information is that your mind is not on your work, and that customers have complained about your attitude to them.'

Laura's eyes flashed.

'That old cat, Lady Blent, I suppose. She hates me, and I hate her. There are others like her too. They think they own the earth.'

'Laura!'

'I hate this job too, although you have been kind to me. I was going to give you a week's notice tomorrow anyway. So I had better give it now.'

This was indeed a turning of the tables, and Bentley was rendered almost speechless.

'You – you have another job?' he asked.

'Yes. I know a film man who has promised me a job whenever I like. I could have started next Monday but I thought I should give you a week's notice.'

'But, Laura, do you know anything about this man?'

'Oh yes. I've seen him lots of times. The job will be in London, and I've always wanted to work in London.'

'Hasn't he asked you for a reference, or some kind of recommendation?'

'No. He said it didn't matter.'

During the next week both partners tried to get some further information from Laura, but without success. The woman with whom she lodged was no better informed, and was somewhat relieved when Laura packed her bags and left.

'She'll come to no good. You mark my words,' she said to her neighbour.

It was two months later that Inspector McLean received a visit from a Mrs. Lamson who kept a boarding house in Bayswater. She had come to inform him that a girl who lodged with her had been missing for two days.

'Her name is Laura Lessing,' she said. 'She has been staying with me for six weeks. Age about twenty-one, and very good looking. Not full board – bed and breakfast only. She went out the night before last and has never come back.'

'Does she owe you anything?'

'No. She must have intended to come back, because all her belongings are in her room, and they include some quite nice bits of jewellery.'

154

'What do you know about the girl?'

'Not very much. I know that she came from Basingstoke, where she was employed by a firm called Bentley Brothers who dealt in silver and leather goods. She told me she was shortly going into a film, the production of which had been delayed.'

'Did she give you the name of the film company?'

'No.'

'Do you know any of her friends?'

'No. But a man named Swinton has telephoned her a number of times, and there's a girl named Monica Gwynn with whom she used to go about. I believe the Gwynn girl was for some time employed at the Windmill Theatre.'

'Have you a photograph of Miss Lessing?'

'Not a real photograph – only a picture which appeared in a newspaper. She showed it to me some time ago, and I found it in her room.'

She took from her handbag a large-sized newspaper cutting which showed a group of girls in the finals of a beauty competition organized by the newspaper. In the centre of the group was the winner – holding a cheque in her hand.

'That's Laura,' said Mrs. Lamson. 'She won a hundred pounds.'

McLean said he would retain the newspaper cutting and would do what he could to locate the missing girl.

'I hope you will,' said Mrs. Lamson. 'She was rather a vain creature, but somehow I got to like her.'

II

It was left to Sergeant Brook to do the preliminaries. McLean could not afford to waste time on what might turn out to be nothing but a wild escapade on the part of the missing girl.

'Try to get in touch with the girl Monica Gwynn,' he said. 'The theatre may be able to help you. If you have no luck there drive down to Basingstoke and make inquiries of the firm where Miss Lessing was lately employed.'

Brook was back again in two hours. He had had some

luck and had found Monica Gwynn at a very shabby address in Camberwell.

'Very synthetic,' he said. 'She was employed at that theatre but only in the front of the house. They sacked her because she wasn't satisfactory. She admitted that she knew Miss Lessing, but swore she hadn't seen her for over a week. I asked her if she knew a man named Swinton.'

'What did she say to that?'

'She hesitated a bit and then said she didn't. I'm certain she was lying.'

'Did she say anything about Lessing's prospective film job?'

'No. She just closed up like an oyster. Said that she and Laura had quarrelled, and she had no further interest in her. I got the feeling that she knew quite a lot, but was scared of getting involved.'

For two days there was no news of the missing girl, and then McLean decided he would see Monica himself. Brook drove him to a dilapidated house in Camberwell where the girl rented a flat on the top floor. She came to the door in a dressing-gown and said she was ill and didn't want to be bothered. She certainly looked ill, and McLean detected the odour of gin while she was speaking.

'This may be an important matter, Miss Gwynn,' he said. 'There are some questions which I must ask you.'

'Okay,' she said wearily. 'Come inside.'

She conducted them to a small and untidy sitting-room which was crowded with old junk. The chairs looked as if they would collapse if one sat on them, and the carpet was threadbare.

'How long have you known Miss Lessing?' McLean asked.

'About six weeks.'

'What was she doing in London?'

'Looking for a job I think.'

'What sort of a job?'

'I don't know.'

'But surely she must have told you something about herself, and her prospects?'

'Not very much.'

'Did you never meet her friend – Mr. Swinton?'

'I've already told—'

'I know. But was it true? I suggest to you that you do know this man, and that for some reason you wish to conceal the fact.'

'No. I've heard his name mentioned, but that is all.'

'Mentioned by whom?'

'A man in a club I belong to. I don't know his name.'

'What club?'

'The Columbine – in Frith Street.'

'What did he say about Swinton?'

'I heard him say that Mark Swinton had got himself a new girl-friend named Laura Lessing, and that someone should tip her off to watch her step. When I saw Laura again I told her what I had overheard. She flew into a temper and told me to mind my own business.'

'Why didn't you mention that when Sergeant Brook questioned you?' McLean asked.

'I'm not looking for trouble. I've got enough of it already. Anyway, now you know the truth.'

McLean wondered whether he really did. The woman looked capable of telling any lie to suit her convenience. But that evening he and Sergeant Brook visited the 'Columbine' and took particulars of everyone present. They were a queer lot, and none of them seemed to follow any profession. All of them denied any knowledge of a man named Mark Swinton, with the exception of a half-intoxicated woman who said that he was a friend of Paul Roxburgh, a member of the same club.

McLean then demanded the membership book, and there found Roxburgh's name and address. Half an hour later he and Brook were ringing the bell at a small house on the edge of Hampstead Heath. There was no reply and it was soon clear that no one was at home. McLean walked round the side of the house, and found three full milk bottles. Under one of them was a pencilled note on the letter-heading of a dairy. It said:

No reply to bell. Milk discontinued until further instructions.

'Gone away without telling the milkman,' said Brook.

A black cat sneaked up to them and stood by the door, uttering a plaintive mew.

'Gone away and left no entry for the cat too,' mused McLean.

He tried the handle of the door and to his surprise he found it unlatched.

'Curious,' he said. 'I think we'll look inside.'

They passed through the kitchen into a passage which opened into a wide hall. From this three rooms radiated. In the largest room which ran down the side of the house they came upon a horrid scene. On a round table there were three drinking-glasses, and some used bottles of drink. A chair was overturned, and the glass front of a cabinet smashed. On the floor, lying half on his face, was a man with a terrible wound in his head. From the congealed blood around the wound it was clear that he had been dead for days. The curtains at the wide casement window had been drawn hurriedly.

'I hope he isn't Roxburgh, but I fear he is,' said McLean.

III

When the police surgeon arrived his opinion was that the man had been dead three days. A dog iron from the fireplace was presumed to be the weapon used, for there were traces of blood on it. This was removed along with the glasses and bottles by the fingerprints crew. In the meantime the victim had been identified by a neighbour as Paul Roxburgh. She knew nothing about the man beyond the fact that he lived with his sister, who had gone on holiday a week previously, leaving him to fend for himself.

When the body had been removed McLean and Brook continued their investigation. The removed glasses, and some ash-trays told part of the story. There had been lipstick on one of the glasses, and now McLean found similar lipstick on half a dozen cigarette butts.

'Two men and a woman at a drinking party,' he ruminated. 'It appears to have started quite well, but then something happened which resulted in one of the men killing the other. I want to see that Gwynn woman again. She may be able to help.'

After locking up the house they paid Miss Gwynn their second visit. She was now fully-dressed and heavily made-up.

158

'I want you to render me a service,' said McLean.

She looked at him suspiciously.

'What is it?' she asked.

'I want to see if you can identify a dead man. Is that asking too much?'

'Not a nice job. But why me?'

'It's just possible you may know him.'

With a little more persuasion Miss Gwynn consented, and was driven to the place where the body lay. Pallid and shaking, she took a good look at the face.

'I – I don't think I know him,' she quavered. 'And yet—'

'He was a member of your club – the Columbine.'

'Why, yes,' she gasped. 'He was the man I told you about – who spoke to another man about Laura Lessing and the man named Swinton.'

'Do you still swear that you have never seen Swinton?'

'Yes. Oh, take me away from here. This place is getting me down.'

McLean delivered her at her door, and then went back to the house of the murdered man.

'I thought perhaps that the murder of Roxburgh might be a coincidence, but now I'm sure it isn't. That woman wasn't telling the whole truth. I believe that she is under a threat – that she knows a great deal about Mark Swinton, but is more afraid of him than she is of us. But let's see what correspondence there is here.'

Drawers and cupboards were ransacked, clothing searched, and boxes opened. Some letters and other documents were found, but there was no clue to the mysterious Mark Swinton, and no hint of how Roxburgh made a living, until behind some books which were projecting from a bookcase he came upon two cartons of cigarettes of a well-known brand.

'A lot of cigarettes for a man to hoard,' he remarked.

He removed one of the packets of twenty, which bore the same maker's name as the cartons. It was packed with cigarettes, but these bore no name, and the paper and tobacco were unusual. McLean lit one and sniffed at the smoke.

'Dope,' he said. 'That settles the question of Roxburgh's profession.'

McLean's next move was to examine the flat of the

missing girl, since the possibility of foul play could no longer be disregarded. He took with him a fingerprint man for reasons of his own. There he found no clue to Swinton, but he established that Laura Lessing had practically nothing left in her Post Office savings account.

The fingerprints man found what he was asked to find – some fingerprints of Laura Lessing. These were found on several toilet articles which the girl had used. At Scotland Yard later it was found that they tallied exactly with the fingerprints on the wineglass which was stained by lipstick.

'Now we know – I think – who it was who visited Roxburgh that evening,' said McLean grimly.

'You mean the Lessing girl and Swinton?' asked Brook.

'Everything points to that. The time of her disappearances agrees with the estimated time of Roxburgh's murder. She was present when the murder took place. What happened afterwards has yet to be discovered.'

'If he killed the one he would be almost certain to kill the other – the only witness to his crime,' argued Brook.

'That's a perfectly logical argument,' said McLean. 'But we need proof of that, and we also need Mark Swinton. Our difficulty in tracing him may be due to the fact that it is an assumed name. Roxburgh might have been able to tell us a great deal about him, but his mouth is closed for ever. We have no physical description of him – nothing that will help to find him. Our one hope is Miss Gwynn.'

'But she won't talk. You said so yourself.'

'I'm still of the same mind. But I may be able to enlist her aid by a rather irregular strategem. I think the circumstances warrant it.'

McLean's irregular strategem consisted of a telegram sent to Miss Gwynn. The wording was very brief and dictatorial.

Come to my place eleven o'clock tonight. Very urgent and important. Swinton.

'If I'm wrong in my suspicions nothing will happen, and no harm will be done,' he said. 'If I'm right we may be led to the hide-out of this mystery man.'

The police trap was laid a full hour before the

appointed time to guard against the possibility of the woman having to travel some distance. Contact had been made with her earlier in the evening, and at nine o'clock she had been trailed back to her flat. Now McLean waited for the upshot in a well-positioned car. Another man was on foot, and yet another on a motor cycle.

At half past ten Miss Gwynn was observed leaving the flat. She walked towards the tube station, but before she got there a taxi appeared. She seemed to hesitate for a moment, and then waved her hand, and the taxi drew up.

'I think it's going to work,' said McLean.

The woman entered the taxi which then turned in the wide road and made away. Instantly the car followed, keeping as far distant as possible without losing touch. The trailing ended suddenly after about twenty minutes of very difficult work, when the taxi pulled up outside a tall house at St. John's Wood.

'Drive right past,' said McLean to Brook. 'We're too close. Take the next turning, then stop.'

This was done and McLean hurried out of the car in time to see the taxi driver paid, and the woman enter the house.

'All right, Brook,' he called. 'Drive the car back to the house.'

A minute or two later a sinister-looking man answered McLean's ring at the bell. Before McLean could say a word a man came hurrying down the stairs, with Monica Gwynn close behind him. He stopped at the sight of the visitors.

'Good evening, Mr. Swinton,' said McLean. 'Come right down,'

The handsome dark features of the man relaxed into a smile and then suddenly he whipped out a pistol. But McLean was just a split second quicker. There was a loud report and Swinton dropped his weapon and clapped a hand to his shoulder. Brook went to him and slipped on the handcuffs.

Wincing with pain Swinton was taken into a downstairs room, along with the woman.

While Brook guarded them McLean went over the house. He found an enormous supply of doped cigarettes, and in a top room bound and gagged was Laura Lessing in a state of exhaustion. It was hours later – in a hospital – before she was able to speak.

'Swinton killed Roxburgh,' she whispered. 'Don't know how it started as I was out of the room at the time. When I came back Roxburgh was on the floor, bleeding. I – I tried to escape but Swinton caught me and brought me here in his car. I trusted him, and he had promised to get me into a film. He threatened to starve me to death unless I went at once with him to France. I refused because I've not been a bad girl – only silly – very silly.'

'Was it Monica Gwynn who introduced you to him?' McLean asked.

'Yes, but afterwards she seemed to regret it. She warned me about him, but I wouldn't believe her. She told me he was the head of a dope gang, and begged me to go back where I came from. Can I go – soon?'

'As soon as you are well, and have signed a statement.'

Two weeks later McLean heard that Laura was back in her old post, and behaving admirably.

16

BUT for the feud between Ralph Mayhew and Wallace Hart the head office of Stewart & Stewart, shipping agents of Fenchurch Street, London, would have been a place of almost perfect harmony, for the company treated its staff with the greatest consideration and the staff in return gave a good account of themselves. How the quarrel between the two men started nobody really knew. But it persisted week after week, month after month until all the other members of the staff were sick of it.

'I wish they'd fight it out like the fabulous Kilkenny cats,' said Watkins the manager. 'Of course, it's all Hart's fault.'

'I think you're wrong there,' said the cashier. 'Hart's always been a decent sort of fellow. Up to the day when Mayhew joined the firm he was as docile as a kitten. Somehow Mayhew has offended him, and won't apologize.'

'But Mayhew isn't that sort of man. I've never known him say an unkind word to anyone. I wish we could find the cause of this friction. We might be able to straighten things out.'

'Why not ask one of the female staff?' suggested the cashier slyly.

'You surely don't think it's some silly love affair, right on our doorstep?'

'That's the only thing which makes sense.'

'But, my dear chap, Mayhew is married. What's more he is very happily married, as I happen to know.'

'Then it's just mutual cat and dog hate. Perhaps they smell bad to each other.'

The manager frowned. He didn't like facetiousness any more than he liked the atmosphere to be poisoned by the antics of Messrs. Hart and Mayhew.

'It's gone on too long,' he said. 'I'm going to put a stop to it, even if one of them has to go to the Liverpool branch.'

But before the manager could put his plan into operation a dreadful thing happened. The body of Mayhew was found in the narrow lane outside the cottage where he lived in Surrey. Inspector McLean was called into the case early, and went at once to the mortuary where the body lay.

'He was brought in last night at ten o'clock,' said the doctor. 'I found that he had been dead about an hour. Fractured skull – left side. I think a short piece of lead piping was used.'

The body was uncovered and McLean looked down on a man of about thirty-five. The hair was sandy and he had a short well-trimmed moustache. He had been dressed in a pair of grey flannel trousers and a sports coat. On the soles of the shoes was a quantity of thick mud.

'So you think he was struck down at about nine o'clock?' asked McLean.

'Within a margin of a quarter of an hour either way. He could not have survived that injury for more than half an hour.'

A little later McLean and Sergeant Brook were in the lane which led to the dead man's house. Here they found a local police officer guarding the actual spot where the body had lain. Some sand had been scattered over the bloodstains on the road.

'I was present when the body was taken away, sir,' said the officer. 'He was lying with his head towards the cottage, which you can just see from here.'

McLean looked ahead and saw the red-bricked cottage about a hundred yards farther on. Abreast of the bloodstains to the left was a large elm tree, but nowhere was there any mud such as that on the dead man's shoes. He did not linger long, but went on to Maple Cottage, where he and Brook were given admittance by the distracted widow. She seemed to be some years younger than her husband, but was as dark as he was fair, with fine features and expressive eyes, now very tearful.

'Tell me what happened last night, Mrs. Mayhew?' asked McLean.

'My – my husband had been working in the garden all day. He loved to do that on fine Sundays. We had a light meal at seven o'clock, and at about eight o'clock he said he felt like a stroll. He asked me if I would go with him, but I had some work to do. I was surprised when it grew dark and he had not returned. Then the police came – told me—'

She broke down and sobbed for a little while. McLean waited for her to recover.

'Do you know of any reason at all why anyone should want to harm him?' he asked.

'No.'

'What was his occupation?'

'He was employed by Stewart & Stewart, shipping agents, of Fenchurch Street. He went there two years ago. Before that he was in another shipping firm but in an inferior position. Of late he hasn't been very happy. I don't know why.'

'How long have you been married?'

'Seven years. I was married soon after my husband came out of the army.'

McLean's gaze went to the piano on which stood a photograph of the dead man. He was in military uniform and bore a captain's badges.

'Any children?' he asked.

'No.'

'You said that of late he wasn't very happy. When did you first notice that?'

'About six months ago, but I think it could have

started much earlier, although I wasn't made aware of it.'

'Did you never ask him what was the matter?'

'Yes, but he denied there was anything wrong. I thought it might be some trouble at the office, but he said he was doing very well there, and in fact soon afterwards he got a nice rise in his salary.'

When it seemed obvious 'that Mrs. Mayhew could throw no useful light on the tragedy, McLean went to the offices of Stewart & Stewart and saw the manager who at that moment knew nothing about what had happened, and presumed that Mayhew's absence from the office was due to illness.

'Murdered!' he gasped. 'How terrible!'

McLean mentioned Mrs. Mayhew's statement that her husband had appeared to be far from happy recently, and asked if the manager had the same impression. Here Mr. Watkins looked very embarrassed.

'Yes,' he said finally. 'There has been some friction here between Mayhew and another member of the staff. I'd better tell you as much as I know.'

II

McLean listened while Watkins related what had transpired. Explaining that nobody in the office had the slightest idea of the cause of the feud.

'I should like to see Mr. Hart,' said McLean.

Hart was called into the room, and after introducing him the manager discreetly retired. Hart was a well-built fellow, several years younger than the dead man, and of a rougher type. He said he had been with the firm three years before Mayhew joined it.

'Was he your superior?' asked McLean.

'Yes.'

'Is it true that you and he were on very bad terms?'

'Yes.'

'What was the cause of that?'

Hart shrugged his shoulders.

'We just didn't like each other,' he said.

McLean wasn't at all satisfied, for it was perfectly clear to him that Hart was concealing the truth.

'I think you should give a more concise answer, Mr.

Hart,' he said. 'For I have to inform you that last night Mayhew was attacked and killed near his home.'

Hart stared at him incredulously, and his face went pallid as he realized the import of the questions.

'I'll tell you,' he said. 'I hated him because some time after he came here I learned that it was he who caused my brother to be degraded and ruined. He was an officer in my brother's army unit, and my brother was a young sergeant. He brought a charge against my brother and at the court martial he got away with it. My brother lost his stripes and was sent to a military prison. But the charge wasn't true. Mayhew had a grudge against him.'

'What became of your brother?' asked McLean.

'He did not come out of prison until the war was over. He swore he wouldn't stay in this country for a moment longer than he could help, and shortly afterwards he emigrated to Canada. A year ago he was killed in a car accident.'

'Did you tell Mayhew that you were the brother of the man he charged?' asked McLean.

'Yes. He said he had only done his duty, and that my brother was found guilty on the evidence.'

'Have you ever threatened Mayhew?'

'Of course not. But I didn't like working with him, and he knew it.'

'Where were you yesterday evening – from seven o'clock onwards?'

'I was at a cinema from half past six until close upon nine o'clock. Then I went to my diggings at Richmond.'

'Were you alone all that time?'

'Yes.'

'So you have no means of proving you were at the cinema?'

'No.'

'Do you know where Mayhew lived?'

'Somewhere in Surrey, but I don't know exactly where.'

McLean could do no more at the moment. It was clear that Hart had no alibi, but it was on the face of it to his credit that he had not attempted to hide his dislike of Mayhew, unless he suspeced that Mayhew's wife knew about the incident of the court martial, in which case it would have been bad policy not to have disclosed it.

'His plea that he didn't know where Mayhew lived

won't hold water,' said McLean to Brook. 'For Mayhew's address must be somewhere in the office. All the same I can't believe that he would carry his dislike so far as to commit murder. Now I want to go back to the scene of the crime. But we'll see Mrs. Mayhew again first.'

On being questioned Mrs. Mayhew said she knew nothing about Hart, nor the court martial of his brother. 'My husband didn't talk much about his army experience,' she said.

'I want, if possible, to find out where your husband went on his walk,' he said. 'Can you suggest any favourite route which he might take?'

'I think he may have gone up to Blackheath, and then back by the field path which comes out in our lane – over the stile. It's a nice circular walk and we used often to do it. I remember—' She stopped and brushed away a tear. 'I remember now that when he asked me to join him he mentioned having a drink on the way, as we had run out of drink in the house.'

'Where would he be likely to stop for that?' asked McLean.

'The Wheatsheaf, I think. That's only ten minutes' walk from here.'

McLean thanked her and then asked if he might borrow the photograph of Mayhew. With this in his pocket he and Brook walked into the lane, and soon reached the spot where the body had been found. The watching police officer was no longer there.

'At nine o'clock it was nearly dark,' mused McLean. 'Mayhew was struck from behind. He could have been overtaken from the rear, but on this rough surface I fancy he would have heard footsteps coming from behind. More likely the murderer had seen him go out but for some reason dared not molest him then. He might have decided to wait until Mayhew came back, and that big elm would give excellent cover.'

The tree grew on a portion of green verge, where the grass was long and thick. No footprints were expected nor found, but it was significant that in the deep grass no less than three cigarette butts were found, and one of these an inch and a half long.

'There, I think, is the proof,' said McLean. 'Two cigarettes were fully smoked, but the third one was only half-smoked when Mayhew was observed approaching. The waiting man pinched it out and threw it away.'

'No name on them,' said Brook scrutinizing the cigarette butts. 'Oh, they're hand-rolled.'

'Yes. Take care of them, especially that pinched one. From here I can see the stile mentioned by Mrs. Mayhew, and a footpath going across the field. We'll cross by the stile.'

They had to walk only about fifty yards to get to the stile. The footpath was well used, and comparatively dry until they reached a five-barred gate, through which cattle had been driven. Here there was so much mud it was impossible to avoid it.

'Mayhew came this way,' said McLean. 'I think I can see the signboard of a public house across that long field.'

On crossing the field the name of the 'pub' came into view. It was The Wheatsheaf, and it looked very much as if Mrs. Mayhew's guess was correct. McLean looked into several bars, and then entered one which was empty. The landlord himself came to serve them, and McLean showed him the photograph of Mayhew and asked him if he had seen the man the previous evening, round about nine o'clock.

'No,' said the landlord. 'We were very busy at that time. Always have a big crowd here Sunday evenings. But my barmaid might remember.'

The barmaid couldn't make up her mind.

'He's been here,' she said. 'Sometimes with a lady, but I can't say that I remember him last evening. We were so busy we coudn't hardly think.'

McLean had to be satisfied with that. Actually it made little difference whether Mayhew had called there or not, but he always liked to get the picture clear, and it was in process of clearing.

III

The next day he saw Hart, not at his place of business but at his lodgings when he returned from work.

'Mr. Hart,' he said. 'You have stated that your brother went to Canada, after his release from prison, and died there from an accident.'

'Yes.'

'How did you get that information?'

'A friend of my brother wrote to me from Toronto, and told me.'

'Have you the letter?'

'No. It was a year ago.'

'What was your brother's last address in Canada?'

'Some address in Toronto. He only wrote about twice in all the time he was there.'

'Did you not receive a certificate of his death, or any communication from a solicitor in regard to any property he may have left?'

'No. I don't think he had any property.'

'Do you not know where he was buried?'

'I did at the time, but I can't remember.'

All this was very unsatisfactory, for it looked as if Hart did not wish to remember. Then McLean asked a question which he could not dodge.

'What was your brother's military unit?'

Hart gave it, along with his brother's full name, and McLean started on a new angle. He searched military records and found that Hart's story was correct. His brother – Herbert – had been before a court martial and sent to a military prison, but one thing Hart had omitted and that was that his brother, prior to going to Canada, had committed robbery in London, and was sent to an ordinary prison for twelve months.

'This may help, Brook,' he said. 'That discarded half-cigarette is yielding some fingerprints at the pinched end, but it's a ticklish job. In the meantime I've asked for Herbert Hart's fingerprints from the record department. They should be with us very shortly.'

'You think he may not be dead?' asked Brook.

'It's possible. We have only his brother's word for it.'

The fingerprints from criminal records arrived in quick time, but still the laboratory were engaged in their very difficult task of reproducing the very faint impressions on the thin cigarette paper. But at last the prints came. They showed parts of a thumb and an index finger, which could have been either right or left hand. They were broken and faint, but good enough to prove the point. McLean compared them with the prison set. They were utterly different.

'Bunkered!' said Brook.

McLean made no comment. His logical mind was now working very fast, and he had to change his ground a little. The circumstances too had changed. It had looked as if Hart was trying to shield his brother, who might conceivably have harboured a long-delayed revenge for an alleged wrong, but now the brother was proved to have been a bad character, and Hart must have known it. The whole case looked different.

Later that day McLean saw various members of the firm of Stewart & Stewart, and obtained answers to innumerable questions which he had noted down, and when finally he returned to Scotland Yard there was a look of achievement on his features.

'I think we've got him, Brook,' he said.

'Hart's brother?'

'No. I've pushed him out of the picture. I mean Hart himself.'

'But I thought you had more or less ruled him out. It seems unbelievable that he should murder a man because of a wrong done to his brother in the distant past.'

'You're right. No wrong was done, but Hart wanted us to believe that was the reason why he disliked him, to prevent us from seeking other causes. He hated Mayhew because before Mayhew came to the firm he believed that he was sitting pretty to become the head of his department. But Mayhew outshone him completely and gradually Hart's chances of ever realizing his ambition faded. His hate grew worse, and only a few days ago he learned that he was being transferred to the Liverpool branch of the firm. It was then I think he went mad. Just one other point. Hart for some time has been trying to give up smoking, but when his nerves are on edge his resolution breaks down. Moreover, he always rolls his own cigarettes. I want you to go along and ask him to come here and have his fingerprints taken.'

'What if he objects?' asked Brook.

'In that case I shall apply for a warrant for his arrest.'

'Shall I tell him the purpose for which he is required?' asked Brook.

'No. We'll tell him when he comes – if he does.'

Brook was out a long time on this quest, but finally he came back with Hart. He had evidently been drinking heavily, and it affected his speech. When McLean told him politely that he wished to have his fingerprints taken he laughed foolishly as if the idea was a joke. But the imprints were taken, and he waited in McLean's office while the results were scrutinized. He asked if he could smoke, and Brook said he could, and watched him while he rolled a cigarette very dexterously. He was about to light it when he stopped and stared into space as if he were seeing visions. The hand which held the lighter trembled visibly, and he dropped it.

'Something troubling you?' asked Brook, as he retrieved the lighter.

Hart seemed quite incapable of speech, and slipped the lighter back in his pocket, without using it. Then McLean came back, and Hart stared into his face.

'I am going to arrest you, Hart, for the murder of Ralph Mayhew,' said McLean.

Hart gave a little choke and the cigarette fell from his fingers on to the carpet. He stared at it, closed his eyes and wrung his hands together.

'All right,' he muttered. 'All right!'

17

THE Barchester Canal mystery started in a curious way, and what promised to be a first-class storm in a tea-cup developed into one of the most perplexing crime cases of the year.

The canal was a stretch of water which started a few miles above Barchester and made junction with a small river some twenty-odd miles to the south. In its heyday it had served as a connecting link between two waterways, and presumably had paid the cost of its excavation and upkeep. But the changing methods of transport had made it derelict, and it was now the property of a single individual named Arthur Walsh, who derived some sort of income from it by supplying water to a local authority and snatching an occasional fee from enthusiastic explorers of inland waterways. But now even the latter source of income was drying up, and only the abundant springs in the bed of the canal made it of any use at all.

Except for the few people who lived in its vicinity the canal was a place forgotten by God and man. Unattended, its banks became like a tropical jungle, and in places almost completely enclosed the narrow reaches.

Two young men looking for new worlds to conquer found a short section of the canal, and were intrigued by its wild beauty. They marked it down as the site of a holiday which they had agreed to spend together, and proceeded to make inquiries as to navigability and charges.

The owner of the canal assured them that it was navigable for its entire length, and quoted a fee of ten shillings for the right to use their small boat on it for one week. The two young men agreed the fee, and a few weeks later they started off in a ten-foot dinghy equipped with a small outboard motor. After travelling a mile or two the propeller became fouled with weed, and rowing had to be resorted to. Then, towards evening, even rowing became impossible and a tow-rope had to be used.

For miles the surface of the water was completely covered by water-lilies and other aquatic plants, and by the time they camped for the night they were worn out. But they hoped the worst was over and that the next day would present open water and good prospects. But they were disappointed, and what should have been made a pleasure was a penance. By sticking it out, and always hoping for something better, they made their objective on the evening of the third day.

Neither of them was prepared to face the return journey by water, and they took steps to have the boat collected and put on the railroad. The cost of this in addition to their own fares home induced them to write a strongly worded letter to the owner of the canal, demanding the fee back, in view of the fact that they had been misled by the statement that the canal was navigable the whole way. The owner quibbled – maintaining that they had exaggerated the difficulties – and still withheld the fee.

The young men, in righteous indignation, informed

the owner that unless he returned the ten shillings they would put the matter in the hands of a solicitor. Tempers were now badly frayed, and a solicitor was consulted. Acrimonious correspondence went on, and finally the solicitor suggested they should get expert opinion regarding the navagability of the canal before taking more drastic action. The outraged young men agreed, and a well-known surveyor and land agent was asked to take the small boat up the derelict waterway.

It was then that the squabble about ten shillings faded into the background, for at a spot about three miles south of Barchester the surveyor, stuck amid millions of water-lilies was compelled to disrobe and make an attempt to wade to the bank, with a towline in his hand. While doing this he endured the unspeakable horror of treading on a dead body. He and his young assistant cleared away a patch of the overgrowth, and through four feet of clear water saw not one body but two – roped together at the bottom of the canal.

In one night the Barchester Canal emerged from its half-century of obscurity and was splashed across the headlines of newspapers. The victims were a man and a woman – totally unrecognizable. They were roped together at the wrists, and round the waist of the man was fastened a heavy chain. The case was too much for the county police, and Scotland Yard was asked to take over the matter.

McLean had never heard of the Barchester Canal prior to this grim discovery. On the best maps it was shown merely as a wriggling blue line, which seemed to make a habit of avoiding all villages and roads.

On arriving at Barchester McLean had an interview with the police officials, and then with the two doctors whom the police had called in. The doctors were in agreement on every point. Death had not been due to drowning but to head injuries inflicted, in both cases, by a curious implement which left deep round holes in the two skulls. The left wrist of the man was broken. Death was presumed to have taken place between three and four months previously. The man's age was estimated to be thirty-two and the woman's twenty-eight. The woman had undergone an operation for appendicitis about three years before the tragedy.

In neither case was there anything in the pockets of the clothing to aid identity. The man wore a dark-brown suit with thin stripes, and the woman a two-piece costume. No hats were found.

'Looks like a long job,' said Sergeant Brook. 'Have we got to see the remains?'

McLean nodded grimly, and later they were taken to the place where the bodies lay. When that part of the investigation was over McLean was relieved. The clothing, which had been dried and disinfected, was taken away, and then McLean and Brook borrowed the surveyor's boat and went to the site of the discovery.

The canal at this point was thirty-five feet wide, and covered from bank to bank with water-lilies, except for a patch measuring about six feet in diameter, from which the bodies had been taken, and where the dense vegetation had been cut. The water was like crystal, and alive with fish. McLean caught a glimpse of a two-foot pike before it shot away under the lilies. Where the bodies had lain the sand had silted up, and the two deep impressions were very pronounced amid the many roots of plants.

They had brought a few cutting implements with them and proceeded to cut away the lilies over a fairly wide area. After two hours of labour the water was clear from bank to bank over a twelve-foot strip. Two old cans were removed, but these had obviously been on the bottom for years. Nothing else was found, and McLean was left with nothing but the original exhibits – the clothing, the length of chain, and a yard of rope.

He consulted the large-scale map which he had brought with him, and found that the nearest habitation was five hundred yards along the north bank. It was a farm of some hundred acres, called Fordings. The next place was a mile along the south bank, and also down stream. It was an inn called The Marigold, and its meadows had an outlet on the canal. Three miles farther south was a village through which the canal actually ran.

'It's an open question whether the victims were brought here by boat or by land,' mused McLean. 'One of the first things to do is to find out what permits have been issued during the past four months. Walsh can give us that information. If the bodies were thrown into the water from the bank, it was certainly on the south side, for they were much nearer that side, and there's scarcely any flow of water.'

Brook agreed, and McLean then moored the boat on the south side of the canal, and began to walk along the bank – downstream. The old towpath was now much overgrown, and progress was slow. After half a mile of scrambling through bushes they came upon an open stretch of water. The bank, too, was less overgrown, and merged into undulating meadows. Suddenly McLean stopped and went off at a tangent for a few yards. He halted under some trees where there was a shallow depression. Here he saw signs of a fire having been lit at some comparatively recent date. The ashes had all been scattered, but he found a number of short sticks with charred ends, and under a bush he discovered two old empty tins and part of a newspaper. The latter was brown with age, but the bush had preserved it to some extent.

'No date,' he muttered. 'That's a nuisance. Still, we may be able to get it. Yes, here's part of the entertainment guide. This is in your line, Brook. Take a look at this list and date it if you can.'

Brook was puzzling this out when McLean saw a paragraph on the back of the page.

'The Monkhouse Wedding,' he said. 'That settles it. Young Lord Monkhouse was married in May – early in May.'

II

It was premature to link the camp-fire with the double murder, but the date coincided nicely and McLean had an interview with the canal owner, who had good records of all the people who had used the canal – legitimately.

'Could one use it without obtaining permission?' asked McLean.

'Well, yes. They'd run a risk of being seen, of course.'

'What licences were issued about that date?'

'Only two. Here's the first – Mr. P. Lyam, of Streatham – a canoe on May the eighth. I remember him, as he came to see me personally. He took his wife. The other is a

Mr. Hewitt. That was done through the post. He started at the lower end on May the fourteenth There was nothing else until June – the second week.'

McLean took both the addresses, and quickly found the two sets of people. Lyam and his wife were charming newly-weds, and had enjoyed the trip. The canal had not been so overgrown at the date on which they had used it, but they had experienced trouble in the part where the bodies had been found. They had not camped at the spot where McLean had found the tins and the newspaper. Mr. Hewitt had made the journey in a punt with two men friends. They had intended camping, but the weather had turned out wet, and they had stayed at the village some three miles away from the site of the camp fire.

'A wash-out,' said McLean to Brook. 'Assuming they are telling the truth. We've got to concentrate on identification.'

This was a difficult problem. A number of people came forward at the request of the police, but went away without being able to help. In view of the circumstances photographs were impossible. The local police assisted by innumerable inquiries about missing persons in the district – all to no purpose.

McLean paid a visit to the farm called Fordings. It was run by a man named Norman and his son. Norman's land extended to the canal, and the fire had actually been lighted on his land. He said he often gave people permission to camp there, but he could not remember having done so at any time in May. The farm was so placed it was impossible to see the canal from it, or a fire lighted where McLean had found the remains. He knew of no missing persons in the neighbourhood.

The proprietor of the Marigold inn often had people putting up with him from off the canal. He recalled Mr. Hewitt, but found no entries in his book for any other persons round about that date. The inquiries went on and McLean began to lose hope. When things were at their worst a woman named Mrs. West, who kept a small private hotel at Wimbledon, came to McLean and said she had read the details of the two victims and believed they were a Mr. and Mrs. Rogers, who stayed with her for a few days in May. She brought a snap-shot of herself and her guests taken in the garden. These included Mr. and Mrs. Rogers. McLean was given this snap-shot, and fresh hope was reborn. Despite the terrible state of the bodies he detected a strong resemblance. But interment had now taken place, and it was impossible for the woman to see them. There was, however, the clothing. The various soiled and torn garments were brought to the woman.

'Why, yes,' she said. I've seen these before.'

'Did the woman ever mention an operation?'

'Yes. She told me she had very nearly died under it. But that was before she was married.'

'What do you know about them?'

'Not very much. I thought they were from the Colonies, because the man was so bronzed. They never talked much about themselves.'

'When did they leave your place?'

'On May the sixteenth.'

'Did they take any luggage?'

'Oh yes – three suitcases in all.'

'Did they give you any idea where they were going?'

'No. They paid the bill and said they liked the house. I thought they were going to London.'

'Why?'

'The woman was always saying she found Wimbledon dull.'

'Can you remember what her husband called her – I mean by what Christian name?'

The woman wracked her memory.

'I'm sorry,' she said. 'I've heard him call her a hundred times, but can't remember what it was. I know it was very short.'

'Did the man sign the visitors' book?'

'Oh yes.'

'I want that signature. If you can think of the woman's Christian name let me know.'

Although some progress had been made McLean felt he was yet a long way from a solution. They had obviously come to the canal in a boat – and without a permit. Where had the man got the boat? If he had borrowed it, where did he get it from and why had the lender not informed the police that the boat had not been returned? Also, where was the boat now?

These questions troubled him for some time. Neighbouring boat-builders were questioned, but none of them had suffered any loss that season. Then McLean got an idea.

'I'm going to the place where we found the signs of the camp fire,' he said. 'I've just remembered something.'

They took the car to the nearest possible place, and then walked over some meadows. On arriving at the spot where he had found the traces of the fire, McLean suffered a disappointment. It had recently been cleared up. One could not even see where the fire had been.

'That's very curious,' mused McLean.

'Why, sir?'

'I wanted particularly to have a look at those charred pieces of wood.'

'Would they help?'

'They might.'

'Well, the farmer may still have them. If he cleaned up the site he may have put them into a dustbin?'

'Why should he clear up the site? It wasn't a great eyesore. All that remained were those few oddly shaped pieces of burnt wood. Perhaps he had a good reason.'

'Eh?'

'If those pieces of wood were all that remained of a burnt rowing boat.'

Brook gave a low whistle as he seized upon the significance of this remark.

'She we go and ask him?' he said.

'Oh no. I think we'll ask him nothing – yet.'

McLean's next step was to find out every possible fact about Norman and his son. It was soon established that he had bought Fordings less than two years before, and that he came from Norfolk. There he had owned a farm of about the same size, and a possible reason for his selling it was that his wife had died there. The son – George – did not help his father run the Norfolk farm, and had only come there after the death of his mother. Witnesses said that George was a bit of a scapegrace, and some believed that he had been sent abroad because of his quarrelsome nature. None of them remembered him as a boy, but as Norman came to Norfolk at a time when George would have been eighteen years of age, it was assumed that George had been packed off before this, and had only come back home after the death of his mother.

'George is a bit of a puzzle,' said McLean. 'He's not a bit like his father – in any way. The old man has a completely different type of face, and is a sober, hard-working type. I want some more information about George.'

<h3 style="text-align:center">III</h3>

Other witnesses were found, and these complicated matters considerably. Two of them mentioned a daughter who had been married to a man abroad about five years before. They gave her name as Rhoda, and McLean was able to establish this fact.

'Anyway, she can't have anything to do with it,' said Brook.

'Can't she? Look at this snap-shot.'

He showed Brook the small snap-shot which the keeper of the lodging house had given him. Brook quizzed it.

'What do you want me to look at?' he asked.

'The woman – Mrs. Rogers. Don't you see something familiar in the nose, and the general make-up?'

'No. Can't say I do.'

'Then you are very unobservant. Every time I look at her I can see Farmer Norman.'

'By jove, you're right!' said Brook. 'I can see it now you point it out. It's his daughter.'

'Not too fast! Ring up Mrs. West.'

The good lady was quickly on the other end of the line. McLean spoke to her and reminded her of Mr. and Mrs. Rogers.

'Did Mr. Rogers call his wife Rhoda?' he asked.

'Why, yes. Sometimes he shortened it to "Ro". But I've heard him call her Rhoda many times.'

'Thank you!'

'This gets worse,' complained Brook. 'If the murdered woman was Norman's own daughter, why should he want to murder her and her husband? It isn't natural.'

'Never mind what's natural. Answer that telephone.'

The caller was a man who lived on the river into which the canal flowed. His attention had been called to certain

179

statements in the Press concerning the double murder, and he was convinced that he had seen the two victims. In May he had advertised a dinghy for sale, and a Mr. and Mrs. Rogers came to see it. They had finally bought it for six pounds, and Rogers had taken it away on 17th May. Rogers had told him that he and his wife were starting a water holiday the next day.

McLean ran down to this new witness, and he had no trouble identifying the couple by the snap-shot which McLean showed him. Where the boat had been stored that night he didn't know, but he had got the impression they were going up the canal.

'What made you think that?' asked McLean.

'He mentioned the canal, and I told him the dues were rather high. He couldn't believe that one had to pay dues to row a boat up a canal, but I told him it was private water.'

'You are sure about the date?'

'Quite sure. You see, he told me he was going to camp out, and on the following night – no, that's wrong, it was two nights later – we had a terrific thunderstorm, which lasted three hours. I thought of them at the time and wondered how they'd get on, because the rain was heavy enough to get through anything.'

This last piece of news was particularly interesting to McLean. It filled in a gap in a rapidly developing theory, but there was still a big snag.

'It's like a tricky crossword puzzle, with no word to fit the last gap,' he said. 'I think I know what drove those two people to the farmhouse, but in that case it brings in a tremendously big coincidence. I don't like coincidences, but it looks as if I've got to accept this one.'

'What is it?' asked Brook.

'That Rhoda Norman and her husband were driven to seek shelter in her father's house, without knowing he lived there. There's no other alternative. She would never have gone there had she known the truth.'

'I can't see why not.'

'Come along to Fordings and you'll see why.'

Two hours later they were at the house. Norman was out but his son was about.

'Did you want father?' he asked.

'Yes, but you'll do,' replied McLean. 'May we come in?'

'Oh yes. This way.'

In the hall were a number of curious relics of South Seas origin.

'Your father was a traveller?' asked McLean.

'Oh no. He's never been out of England. It was his brother who sent those home. He was a farmer in Australia.'

McLean noted the term 'his brother'. It wasn't usual for men to speak in that way of their uncle. They passed into a very fine old room, and McLean produced his note-book.

'You had a sister?' he asked suddenly.

'Me? Oh yes – Rhoda of course.'

'Where is she now?'

'In Canada. She went out there to marry a man.'

'What was his name?'

'Hawkins.'

'How long ago was that?'

'About five years.'

'Have you a photograph of her?'

'N-no.'

'You mean to say you've not a single photograph of your own sister – not even a snap-shot?'

'No. We had some, but they've got lost.'

'Allow me to show you one,' said McLean, and produced the snap-shot.

The young man went pale as he stared at the photograph. McLean watched him like a lynx. His breath was coming in jerks and his hand trembled slightly.

'That's her,' he said. 'Where did you get it?'

'Is that her husband next to her?'

'Yes. I thought they were both in Canada.'

'Who says they're not?' snapped McLean.

'Well, it doesn't look like Canada.'

'How do you know what Canada looks like. Oh yes, you've been there, haven't you?'

'Yes.'

'In fact you married Rhoda Norman in Canada, didn't you? To be even more precise, you are Mr. Hawkins and not the son of John Norman at all?'

'That's a lie!' snapped the young man.

181

'You referred to Norman's brother not as your uncle but as Norman's brother. Are you or are you not John Norman's son-in-law? Be careful how you answer that question, for this is a very serious business.'

The young man gulped.

'I'm George Hawkins,' he said. 'I married Rhoda Norman. She ran away from me. That's all I know. My father-in-law offered me a home with him, when his wife died, and I came home.'

'Have you seen your wife since that date?'

'No.'

It was then the door opened and John Norman entered, and gazed at the party.

'Sit down, Mr. Norman,' said McLean. 'Tell me why you passed off your son-in-law as your son?'

The old man look flustered.

'I – I always thought of him as my son,' he said.

'When did you last see your daughter – alive?'

Norman shook his head, and pressed his hand to his heart. It was clearly no trick, and McLean asked the son-in-law if there was any brandy in the house.

'In the dining-room,' he said, and made to leave.

'No, I'll go,' snapped McLean.

He went across the hall and found a decanter with some brandy in it. But he found something else too, balanced on two nails in the wall. It was a native implement fashioned out of exceedingly hard wood. It was like a battle-club, and two inches from the heavy end of it a piece of metal had been forced through it. It protruded about an inch and a half, and was just such a weapon as had caused the wounds in the heads of the two victims. McLean took this with him as well as the decanter.

Immediately he entered the other room Hawkins's gaze went to the implement. He said nothing, but when McLean was administering the brandy he made a sudden leap for the door and got through it. He was finally rounded up in the meadow, and succumbed only after a bitter and stupid fight in which half his teeth were knocked out by Brook. When they returned to the room they had left the old man had revived.

'It's no use,' he said to McLean. 'I've had no sleep since it happened. I'll tell you everything. I'm a God-fearing man and this has laid on my soul too long. The poor boy was demented. He didn't know what he was doing. I had to shield him – for a bit – but now I'm glad there will be no more lies.'

His story was much what McLean expected. His daughter had been attracted to another man in Canada, and finally she had left her husband. Hawkins had taken to drink, and was ruining himself. Old Norman knew this and invited him home. Hawkins had never ceased to remember his wife and the man who had wrecked his happiness. On that particular evening, when the great storm had broken, Norman was in the village, unable to get home. When he did come home he found his dead daughter and Rogers. Hawkins told him how they had come there for shelter. He had gone mad at the sight of them and had struck at them with the first available implement. The man had put out his arm to ward off a blow, but had failed to prevent the terrible ending.

'It was Providence,' moaned the old man. 'It led her and him to their doom. George was a fine man until she left him. I don't want to speak ill of her, but she drove poor George out of his mind. I helped him burn the boat, and destroy everything else. To that extent I'm guilty. We took them in a wheelbarrow away from my land and sunk them where I thought the water-lilies would cover them for ever. That's all I have to say.'

It was enough to make the case a very easy one when it was tried.

18

THE little quiet man in the little quiet cottage at Pryke in the county of Sussex seemed a bit of an automaton to the other residents of the lovely village. Every day he appeared to do exactly the same thing – took his Sealyham dog for a walk at eleven o'clock in the morning, called at the Huntsman inn round about twelve, where he had a pint of beer and bought some biscuits for the dog. Lunched at one o'clock, thereafter slept until about three, and then pottered in the garden. Mrs. Badger, who was employed by him from eight till five, found the work at the cottage very easy, for he was a scrupulously tidy person, and paid her generously for her services.

'He's a nice man, is Mr. Proctor,' she said. 'Not a gentleman, if you know what I mean. I've worked for gentlemen so-called, and I know. Give me Mr. Proctor any time. No airs and graces with him. The other day I dropped the tea tray, and everything on it was smashed to bits. All Mr. Proctor said was, "Well, Mrs. Badger, I always did dislike that tea service. Now we have an excuse to buy another lot." '

The grocer who was serving her laughed, and then totted up the cost of the groceries on the back of a sugar bag.

'I often see him with that dog of his,' he said. 'Seems very devoted to it.'

'Oh, he is. I don't know what he would do without Peter. He's a very lonely man. Never has any visitors, and few letters. Well, I must get back to prepare his lunch. I've got a nice surprise for him – a recipe I heard on the radio.'

But Mrs. Badger's surprise luncheon never materialized, for at one o'clock, when lunch was always ready to the minute, Mr. Proctor had not returned. This was most surprising, for never in her two years of service at Eden Cottage had Proctor ever been late for lunch. It was at half past two when Peter, the Sealyham, arrived home alone.

'Why, Peter!' she gasped. 'Where's the master?'

The dog's reaction was most unusual. He walked to the door which led into the passage and waited there, looking back at her. Then he barked furiously and came back to her, only to return again to the doorway and wait. It was clear now that he wanted her to follow him, so she slipped off her apron and did so.

The dog bolted through an open casement window, and across the lawn to the gate. Mrs. Badger, who was portly, puffed as she went after him. He led her through lanes and up over the downs until they came to an old chalk pit, the rear wall of which towered a hundred feet and more above the debris in the bottom. She gasped as she saw the dog dash forward and lie prone before a still, human form. A few moments later, tearful and gasping for breath, she stood beside the dead body of Mr. Proctor.

Mrs. Badger hurried to the nearest telephone, and the county police were soon on the site of the tragedy. It was clear that Proctor had fallen from the top of the cliff, but it was difficult to understand how the accident had occurred, for fringing the pit there was a wire fence. The footpath across the downs came within about six feet of the fence, which was undamaged. There was the possibility that Proctor had climbed through the wires to retrieve something, and had then slipped and fallen to his death, and there was in fact a disturbance of the grass on the cliff-top just above the spot where his body had been found.

Then came the result of the very careful medical examination. It was that all the body injuries were consistent with the fall; also damage to the right jaw. But on the right side of the head there was an injury which in the opinion of the two doctors had not been caused by the fall, for inside that wound they had found a very small fragment of wood.

This ominous discovery caused the county police to ask for the assistance of Scotland Yard, and Inspector McLean was sent down to Pryke, with Sergeant Brook. On the way he called at county police headquarters, where he saw an Inspector Danielson, who had had charge of the case. Danielson showed him the minute blood-stained wood splinter.

'If it isn't murder I'll eat my hat,' he said.

'It certainly points that way,' agreed McLean. 'Tell me about the victim. What do you know of him?'

'Not a great deal. I've not even had time to examine his effects, because the moment that splinter came to light the Chief decided to hand the case over. His name is Kenneth Proctor, and he bought Eden Cottage at Pryke about two years ago. A rather meek and inoffensive little man, not particularly well spoken. Round about sixty. Might be a retired grocer or something like that. No knowledge of where he came from before he bought the cottage. A woman named Mrs. Badger, who lives in the village, has looked after him ever since he came to the district. She speaks very well of him, as does everyone else who knew him. Seems to have been comfortably off, but never made any close friends. Wanted to be left alone, and was. Why anyone should want to murder him is a complete mystery.'

'Any known relatives?'

'None.'

'What was the time when the incident is presumed to have taken place?'

'Round about eleven o'clock. I should tell you that it was his custom to take a morning walk with his dog. He never varied his programme, wet or fine. Most people in the neighbourhood would know it, and it looks as if he was waylaid.'

II

McLean finally went on to Eden Cottage, where he found Mrs. Badger taking her 'elevenses' and looking very mournful. She had been told that the case had gone to Scotland Yard, and that she would probably be questioned again.

'I've told all I know,' she said. 'And that isn't much. Mr. Proctor left home about half past ten, with the dog, and then the dog came back alone—'

'I know all that,' said McLean. 'Had there been any telephone calls for Mr. Proctor that morning, or the night before?'

'Not that morning – and I'm not here in the evenings.'

'Has there been any change in his disposition recently? I mean – did he display any unusual signs of worry?'

'Oh no. He was always the same. Very quiet, but cheerful. He was never upset by anything. Never lost his temper or said an unkind word.'

'What about visitors?'

'He never had any – not when I've been in the house. When he first came here the rector called on him – twice I think. But when he found that Mr. Proctor wasn't a churchgoer he didn't come again.'

'Has he never mentioned his past life to you?'

'Not in any detail. Once he told me he had lost his wife just before he came here, and that he couldn't bear to go on living in the same house, because it reminded him too often of her. I think he had a son who was killed in the war, because there is a photograph of a soldier in his bedroom who looks very much like him.'

'What makes you think the son is dead?'

'I found a war medal in a drawer – the last war. Mr. Proctor couldn't have been in that.'

McLean then said he wanted to examine the dead man's personal effects, and Mrs. Badger went back to her kitchen. The sad-looking Sealyham dog followed McLean and Brook to the bedroom which Proctor had occupied, and spread himself on the carpet while they went about their business.

Here McLean had a surprise, for stacked in a little box lying at the back of a drawer were a number of interest vouchers in respect of Government bonds. He whistled as he saw the capital sums printed on the vouchers. Quickly he added up the figures.

'Over sixty thousand pounds!' he said. 'All dated over the past two years. He certainly lived economically for a man of his means.'

In another drawer was a cheque book, and a paying-in book. These and other documents showed that Proctor had his main banking account in London, but kept a drawing account at the Brighton branch of the same bank. The payments into the London bank appeared to be confined to the half-yearly interest of the bonds. The drawings were for regular small sums.

'No income except from his investments,' mused McLean.

'I'd be satisfied with that,' said Brook.

McLean was hopeful of finding a will, but he was unsuccessful in this. There was, however, a file of letters received, and he put these aside for future examination.

'We'll call at the London bank when we get back,' he said. 'They may have a will there. Someone is going to inherit sixty thousand pounds and a nice cottage, and I should like to know who.'

A little later McLean and Brook went to the top of the chalk-pit where Proctor had met his end. It was a deserted spot, for the main paths over the downs were half a mile distant, and only persons who lived in the vicinity would use that particular track, since it led nowhere.

A very careful examination of the ground in the neighbourhood of the disturbed grass convinced McLean that Proctor had been struck down some yards from the wire fence, and that his body had been dragged through the bottom and middle strands of wire, and then pushed over the edge. This was borne out a little later when he succeeded in finding blood stains on the grass.

'That rules out all possibility of accident,' he said. 'It was doubtless planned to look like an accident. But that little splinter of wood in ¡the head-wound, and these few spots of blood are conclusive. Let's go down below.'

They made the steep descent to the entrance at the pit's bottom, and here it was easy to see where the falling man had come to rest, for there was a good deal of blood where it had lain unattended for so long. Here it was all chalk, for the pit had been used up to a recent date, and no grass had grown. McLean walked around, not expecting to find anything of interest. But in this he was wrong, for between the site where the body had lain and the entrance there were traces of blood at intervals of about five feet – two separate series in fact.

'The dead man couldn't have made those,' he said, 'since he was removed on a stretcher. The county police were singularly unobservant.'

'But how did they get here?' asked Brook.

'There's only one answer which makes any sense. I believe the murderer came down here afterwards to make sure that his victim was dead. He had an injury to one of his legs, and every time he took a step with that leg, or almost every time, it shed a little blood.'

'But presumably Proctor was knocked cold. He couldn't have caused any injury to his attacker.'

'You overlook the one witness of this crime – that dog. My impression is that he took a hand in matters, and got in a bite before he was driven off.'

They tried to find more traces of blood outside the entrance to the pit, but were unsuccessful, for here the grass was long and rank. When they finally returned to the cottage the Sealyham was lying on the lawn, head on paws. His short tail wagged just a little as he recognized them as friends. McLean approached him, and was permitted to pat him and to run his hands over the animal's muscular body. When he reached his rump the dog gave a little yelp of pain.

'All right, old boy,' said McLean. 'I'm not going to hurt you.'

Gently he probed into the heavy fur.

'Here it is,' he said. 'A pretty hefty bump. Might be the result of a kick, or a blow from the weapon which killed Proctor. At least we've achieved something.'

When he returned to London McLean took with him the small splinter which had been found in Proctor's head-wound. It was handed to the laboratory for examination and report. His subsequent visit to the bank which kept Proctor's account produced a little more information about the dead man's past.

'He opened an account here two years ago,' said the manager. 'With a seventy-five-thousand-pound cheque from one of the big pools. His address was then at Wimbledon, but he told me later that he had been so worried by hundreds of begging letters that he couldn't face up to it. His wife too had died shortly before he won that big prize, and he wanted to find a place where he could live quietly. It wasn't long before he found that cottage in Sussex. I advised him in the matter of investment, and since then I haven't set eyes on him.'

'Do you know if he made a will?'

'I'm sure he didn't. I did mention that matter to him, in view of his unexpected windfall. He wasn't very keen about it – gave me to understand there was nobody really close to his heart. His wife was dead and he had no children. He was only sixty and in good health. He finally said that there was plenty of time to think about the matter, and he would come and see me if he came to any decision.'

'Did he say definitely that he had no children?'

'Yes.'

'Did he mention any living relatives on his side?'

'No, but I gathered there was no one.'

'Do you know what profession he followed before he won that prize?'

'No. He was not very communicative. A very quiet man with simple tastes. I was even surprised to discover that he had the slightest interest in football pools.'

McLean spent the rest of the evening going through the file of letters which he had taken away. It was soon clear that Proctor up to the date of his windfall had

189

run a little picture-framing business at Wimbledon, and most of the letters dealt with business matters. There was nothing to show that he had any surviviing relatives, or to suggest any reason why he should have been attacked. The coroner's inquest returned the inevitable verdict of murder.

After the failure to locate any will made by the dead man an advertisement in the Press requested next of kin to get in touch with Scotland Yard. Days passed and no response came.

'Looks as if there was no gainful motive,' said Brook. 'Probably revenge for some act performed in the past.'

'Not quite in keeping with his character as we know it. He seems to have been a quiet, inoffensive man,' replied McLean.

'They're a long time working on that wood splinter, aren't they, sir?'

'I've just had a report. Doesn't help much, as the Lab can't identify the wood. Not enough of it for them to arrive at a conclusion. It's a hard wood, probably tropical.'

Then suddenly there came a response to the advertisement. It was a letter from a woman in Ireland, who stated that she was the sister of Proctor, and had married an Irish farmer named Gorman. She was flying to London the next day, and would bring with her proof of her claim.

III

Mrs. Gorman arrived at McLean's office that evening. She was old and poorly dressed, and looked ill. She produced from her handbag her birth certificate, in the name of Grace Proctor, dated sixty-five years earlier, a photograph of the murdered man when he was a mere stripling, and two letters from him, very crumpled and dirty, dated twenty years earlier.

'We weren't on good terms,' she explained. 'I ran away from home when I was eighteen, and my family never forgave me. Years afterwards when I was married to a respectable farmer, and both my parents were dead, I tried to make it up with my brother Kenneth. You can see from these letters that he was embittered towards me, and I can't blame him because then I was a wild and ungrateful girl. Our brief correspondence ended and I saw no more of him.'

McLean read the letters, which bore out her statement, and it seemed to him that she would have little difficulty in proving her claim.

'Did you know that your brother had come into quiet a lot of money?' he asked.

'No. I knew he had a little business, but I didn't think it was one in which he could make much money. I'm sorry about his death. I didn't even know he was ill.'

'Is your husband alive?' asked McLean.

'No. He died fifteen years ago, leaving me with a lad to bring up and educate.'

'Does your son run the farm now?' McLean asked.

'Oh no. I had to sell the farm years ago – to give Michael a good education. He's in banking, and is doing quite well.'

'In Ireland?'

'No – in London. One of the big banks.'

'Which one?' asked McLean.

Sergeant Brook almost collapsed when she named the bank at which the dead brother kept his account. But McLean showed no emotion of any kind.

'I shall have to retain these documents, Mrs. Gorman,' he said, 'until such time as your claim is proven. Will you be staying with your son?'

'Oh no. He only has a small flat. I have booked a room at the Connaught Hotel in Dean Street.'

'I will keep in touch with you,' McLean promised, and then Brook showed Mrs. Gorman out.

It was early the next morning, as soon as the bank was open, that McLean saw the manager.

'Have you a man here named Michael Gorman?' he asked.

'Yes. He has been here five years. He came from Dublin.'

'Is he on the premises now?'

'No. He is on holiday. Due back on Monday.'

'Did you not know that this man is the nephew of Kenneth Proctor?'

The bank manager stared incredulously.

'What an astonishing coincidence!' he said. 'But he never told me. Probably he doesn't know himself.'

'I think he does. What sort of a man is he? Is he completely satisfactory?'

The manager looked down his nose. It was clear he was embarrassed by the question.

'I'm not very happy about him,' he finally admitted.

'Could he by any chance know that Proctor had left no will?'

The manager reflected for a moment.

'He might,' he said. 'I think he was on the counter when Proctor left my office after our discussion about making a will. Proctor's last words to me were, "I'll think about that matter of a will. But there's plenty of time – I hope." He was standing at the open door then, shaking hands.'

That was enough for McLean. He asked for Gorman's address and went to the flat. The place was locked up, but later that day McLean and Brook found Gorman at home. He was a powerfully built fellow of about thirty, and he expressed surprise when McLean revealed his identity.

'What's the trouble?' he asked.

In the little sitting-room the questioning began. He swore he did not know that Proctor was his uncle. He knew that he had had an uncle but believed he was dead. Asked where he had been during his holiday he was a trifle vague. He did not yet know that his mother was in London, nor why she might have come. Satisfied that he was lying McLean then produced a search warrant, and proceeded to investigate the place.

He found an hotel bill from a place only two miles from Pryke covering four days, one of the days being that on which Proctor was killed. Then he found a heavy black stick with a bulbous head. This carved head was slightly splintered, and deep in the carving was something which looked like dried blood. He came back to the sitting-room with the bill and stick in his hand. Gorman now looked terrified and pale as a sheet.

But worse was to come. A personal search revealed a crêpe bandage just above the right ankle. When this was removed it brought to light the clear impressions of a dog's teeth. Speechless, Gorman was taken to the waiting car.